"Where are you going?" she whispered in a sleep-laced voice that triggered images of the two of them in bed together.

"I know it sounds silly," she continued, "but I don't want to be alone."

He didn't want that either. He wanted to make love to her.

Instead, he brushed the pad of his thumb across her cheek. "I'll sleep on the couch," he said, his voice thick and hoarse. "If you need me, just call."

She nodded, closed her eyes again and curled into her bed. He ached to drop a kiss on her cheek, then her mouth, but remembered the doctor's warning about her memory returning at its own pace and forced himself to leave the room.

Still, his body hummed with arousal and a fierce hunger that could only be sated by Aspen.

A woman who saw him as a perfect stranger.

RITA
HERRON

COLLECTING EVIDENCE

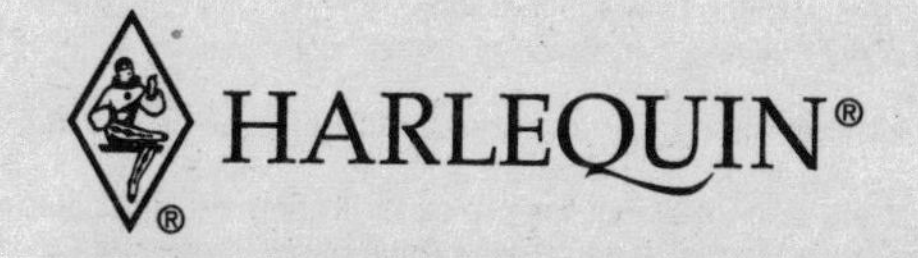

TORONTO • NEW YORK • LONDON
AMSTERDAM • PARIS • SYDNEY • HAMBURG
STOCKHOLM • ATHENS • TOKYO • MILAN • MADRID
PRAGUE • WARSAW • BUDAPEST • AUCKLAND

To Jamie, a brave and courageous young girl—
may all your dreams come true!
Special thanks and acknowledgment
to Rita Herron for her contribution
to the Kenner County Crime Unit miniseries.

Recycling programs for this product may not exist in your area.

ISBN-13: 978-0-373-69399-3
ISBN-10: 0-373-69399-0

COLLECTING EVIDENCE

This edition published by arrangement with Harlequin Books S.A.

www.eHarlequin.com

Printed in U.S.A.

ABOUT THE AUTHOR

Award-winning author Rita Herron wrote her first book when she was twelve, but didn't think real people grew up to be writers. Now she writes so she doesn't have to get a *real* job. A former kindergarten teacher and workshop leader, she traded storytelling to kids for romance, and writes romantic comedies and romantic suspense. She lives in Georgia with her own romance hero and three kids. She loves to hear from readers so please write her at P.O. Box 921225, Norcross, GA 30092-1225, or visit her Web site at www.ritaherron.com.

Books by Rita Herron

HARLEQUIN INTRIGUE

790—MIDNIGHT DISCLOSURES*
810—THE MAN FROM FALCON RIDGE
861—MYSTERIOUS CIRCUMSTANCES*
892—VOWS OF VENGEANCE*
918—RETURN TO FALCON RIDGE
939—LOOK-ALIKE*
957—FORCE OF THE FALCON
977—JUSTICE FOR A RANGER
1006—ANYTHING FOR HIS SON
1029—UP IN FLAMES*
1043—UNDER HIS SKIN*
1063—IN THE FLESH*
1081—BENEATH THE BADGE
1097—SILENT NIGHT SANCTUARY**
1115—PLATINUM COWBOY
1132—COLLECTING EVIDENCE

*Nighthawk Island
**Guardian Angel Investigations

CAST OF CHARACTERS

Aspen Meadows—She has no memory of her past—or the reason someone wants her dead.

Dylan Acevedo—He's determined to find the men who killed his fellow agent and believes Aspen may be the key. But could her lost memories hold secrets that she'd kept from him—like a child?

Baby Jack—Aspen's son. But who is the baby's father, and does his paternity have something to do with the man after Aspen?

Boyd Perkins—did the contract killer try to murder Aspen because she saw him dumping FBI agent Julie Grainger's body?

Sherman Watts—A local Ute man. Is he helping Boyd Perkins hide out on the Ute reservation?

Kurt Lightfoot—A pillar of the Ute community who wanted Aspen for himself. But was he involved in something illegal? And had he tried to kill Aspen because she blew him off?

Frank Turnbull—Dylan thought he'd seen the last of the serial killer who targeted Ute women. But did Turnbull really die or has he escaped and come back for revenge?

Sally Ann McCobb—She wrote Turnbull love letters while he was in prison. Did she help him escape?

Larry Gerome Sawyer—A serial killer who befriended Turnbull in prison. Was his body in the crash?

Ulysses—Is he copying Turnbull's MO?

Prologue

Special Agent Dylan Acevedo pressed the blade of the knife against Frank Turnbull's fleshy neck.

"Go ahead, kill me," Turnbull muttered.

Dylan jabbed the blade into his skin, a smile curving his mouth as a drop of blood seeped to the surface. He should just do it.

The man deserved to die.

The images of the women the serial killer had brutally murdered—all young Native Americans in their twenties—flashed into Dylan's head in sickening clarity. Their delicate throats slashed, bodies left exposed in the rugged terrain of the desert, blood dripping as if to lure the wild animals to feed on their remains.

Young lives lost for no reason except to fulfill the sick cravings of a demented mind.

Dylan glanced down at the knife in his hand. The knife that had belonged to Turnbull. The same kind he'd used to cut the women's throats.

It was only fitting he die by the same instrument.

With his throat sliced open by a Ute ceremonial knife made from white quartz and Western Cedar, the kind of knife used to cut the umbilical cord of a newborn or to harvest herbs for sacred ceremonies.

Another important component of Turnbull's MO was his calling card—he'd left a piece of thunderwood by each victim. Another dig to the Ute people who had a religious aversion to handling thunderwood—a piece of bark from a tree struck by lighting. The Utes believed that thunder beings would strike down any Ute Indian who touched it.

Turnbull's swollen eye twitched with menace and a dare. A challenge to Dylan to feel the thrill of the kill, Turnbull seemed to say silently.

Dylan clenched his jaw. He wanted to see fear in Turnbull's eyes. Wanted to hear him scream as his victims had. Hear him beg for his life.

Instead Turnbull laughed, a hideous deep growl that punctured the night like a wild animal just before it tore into a smaller one's carcass.

"You're just like me," Turnbull mumbled. "I can see the evil in your eyes."

Dylan's fingers tightened on the knife handle. At that moment he did crave the kill. But his need was driven by revenge and justice, not depraved indifference.

"Dylan, don't…."

His brother Miguel's voice rumbled from behind him. Miguel, who was a saint compared to him. He'd been an altar boy while Dylan had been the troublemaker.

They hadn't always gotten along, but as adults they'd forged a bond and developed a healthy respect for one another's differences. Miguel was a forensic scientist, and they often worked together on cases, relying on each other's expertise.

Miguel's footfalls echoed on the ground as he approached. "Come on, Dylan. We've got him. Let's take him in and make him pay for what he did. Make him face the families of the victims."

Dylan's hand trembled as his gaze once again locked with the monster. Then he saw the fear in the man's eyes. Turnbull wanted him to kill him.

Because he didn't want to face the families.

Miguel was right. Having to look into the pain-filled eyes of the parents of the women he'd hurt would be his worst punishment.

His hand slipped, caught the skin just enough to cause a flesh wound, then he gestured for Miguel to cuff the bastard.

HOURS LATER, after their debriefing and a press conference to announce they'd finally arrested the ruthless Ute killer, Dylan walked into the Vegas bar. All he wanted was to purge his rage, and drown out the images of the girls he hadn't been able to save.

Just like he hadn't saved his fifteen-year-old sister, Teresa, when she'd been gunned down in a gang-related drive-by.

Suddenly, the most exotic creature he'd ever seen approached him. Long black hair that hung down to her waist swayed seductively as she walked, her dark chocolate eyes raking over him appreciatively.

She was Ute, fit the profile of the victims he'd fought so hard to obtain justice for. Could have become number eleven on Turnbull's kill card. Yet here she was, alive and smiling at him.

"Agent Acevedo," she said in a purrlike voice with

the faint accent of her heritage. "I saw you on the news. Thank you for arresting that killer."

He shrugged. "I only wish we'd caught him sooner."

Wise, sympathetic eyes met his, along with a sultriness that made his body go rock hard and achy.

He was mesmerized by her beauty, wanted her naked and in his bed, soothing the heat and rage in his soul.

When she finished her shift, they talked for hours. Her name was Aspen Meadows. She was working as a cocktail waitress while earning a teaching degree.

Finally he escorted her to her apartment. Before he closed the door, she was in his arms and he was tearing off her clothes. He took her on the floor, against the wall, on the bed and in the shower.

A week of lovemaking couldn't assuage the pain or guilt in his chest. He didn't deserve her. Didn't deserve to be loved or soothed when he'd failed so many.

But he stole the hours and days anyway, desperate for a slice of heaven to ease the hell he lived with daily.

He knew it wouldn't last, *couldn't* last, though. A phone call the following Friday night reminded him too well.

Another murder. An undercover assignment.

He had to go.

He kissed her goodbye and left while she was sleeping. He wouldn't see her again. He couldn't.

His work put anyone he cared about in danger.

And he had enough dead girls haunting him to last him forever.

Chapter One

A year later

Aspen Meadows had been missing for nine weeks now. Nine weeks of wondering if she was dead or alive.

Nine weeks of wondering if he could have done something to save her.

Dylan stared at Aspen's cousin, Emma Richardson, fearing the worst. He'd left Aspen last year to keep her safe, yet now she might be dead.

Possibly murdered by the same hit man who'd killed his fellow agent, Julie Granger. The FBI's theory—Aspen had witnessed Boyd Perkins and Sherman Watts disposing of Julie's body.

The case that had brought them to the Southern Ute reservation.

Emma pressed a hand to her head as if to clear her vision. "Aspen is alive."

His chest tightened as hope speared him. He didn't often trust a psychic, but Emma's visions had proven right before, and his brother, Miguel, who'd obviously fallen for the woman, believed her wholeheartedly.

And he trusted his twin brother more than anyone in the world.

Still, he had to swallow to make his voice work. He'd prayed for this news ever since he'd heard Aspen's car had been found crashed into a tree near the San Juan River.

But something about the tortured look on Emma's face disturbed him. "Are you sure she's alive?"

Emma nodded, although she swayed, her face pale, her eyes gaunt. Miguel rushed to help her to the sofa. She leaned her head back and closed her eyes with a shudder.

"What did you see?" Sweat beaded on the nape of Dylan's neck. He was terrified that Aspen had died and that he'd lost her forever.

Just as he'd lost almost every woman he'd ever cared about. His little sister, Teresa. Then his friend Julie.

Miguel rubbed Emma's arms, his voice low and worried, "Emma?"

"I...don't know. The vision... I just know she's alive, but she's scared." She opened her eyes and looked up at Dylan, cold terror streaking her expression. "And she's in danger."

Dylan paced across the room, his heart pounding as Aspen's son, Jack, cried out. The sound shattered the air as if he'd heard Emma and understood that his mother might be in trouble. Emma started to rise to go to the baby, but Dylan waved her off. She looked as if she might faint if she tried to stand.

He strode over to the bassinet and picked up the squirming baby. Jack flailed his tiny fists, his face red, his nose scrunched as he continued to bellow.

"Shh, little man," Dylan said, jiggling him on his shoulder as he paced the room. The poor little fellow must miss his mother terribly. In the first few weeks of his life, he'd been in a car accident with Aspen, abandoned and left with Emma.

He patted the baby's back, cradling him closer. The scent of baby powder and formula suffused him.

If Aspen was alive, why hadn't she come back for her son?

The Aspen he'd known loved children more than anything. During their short affair—the best sex of his whole damn life—she'd told him her plans to return to the Ute reservation and teach.

Baby Jack kicked and screamed louder, a shrill sound that added to the tension thickening the room, his dark skin beet-red, contrasting to his thick black hair. He had Aspen's high-sculpted cheekbones, her hair, her heritage. It made Dylan long to see her again, to reconnect and hold her. To see if they could pick up where they'd left off and possibly have more than just a week of mind-boggling sex.

But she had a son now.

Everything had changed.

He rocked Jack back and forth, lowering his voice again to calm him. "Shh, it's all right. We'll find your mommy. I promise, little man."

Jack quieted to a soft whimper and Dylan turned him to his back, cradled him in his arms and gazed into his eyes. Eyes so blue that for a moment he felt as if he was looking in the mirror.

Suddenly a wave of emotion washed over him, sending his mind into a tailspin. He studied Jack's features more closely while he mentally calculated the baby's age, and the time lapse since he'd last seen Aspen. A little over a year ago, they'd met and fallen into bed. A week later he'd left and hadn't heard from her again.

Aspen had been missing now for nine weeks.

Jack was fifteen weeks old.

Dear God, could Jack possibly be his son?

The baby suddenly cooed up at him, his chubby cheeks puffing up as he gripped one of Dylan's fingers in his tiny fist.

Dylan's chest swelled. "Is it true, Jack? Are you my little *mijo?*"

And if he was, why in the hell hadn't Aspen told him?

THE NIGHTMARES TAUNTED HER.

Every night they came like dark shadowy demons with claws reaching for her and trying to drown her in the madness.

If only she could remember her name, what had happened to her, how she had wound up near death and here in this women's shelter in Mexican Hat.

But the past was like an empty vacuum sucking at her, imprisoning her in the darkness. Only at night in her dreams, memories plucked at the deepest recesses of her mind, trying to break through the barrier her subconscious had erected.

Terrifying memories that she wasn't sure she wanted to recall.

She forced herself to look into the mirror, to probe her mind for bits of her past. She knew she was Ute—her high cheekbones, long black hair and brown eyes screamed Native American heritage.

But those eyes were haunted by something she'd seen, something that lay on the fringes of her conscience.

Her head throbbed, tension knotting her stomach. She rolled her shoulders to stretch out her achy muscles, but exhaustion was wearing on her. In the weeks since she'd come to the shelter, she'd recovered from her physical injuries, the hypothermia and bruises, but she still hadn't regained her strength.

The other women and children had gathered after dinner for a support group session in the common room. Sometimes she gathered the children into a circle on the floor for storytime, but tonight one of the mothers was teaching them how to string Indian beads to make necklaces.

Grateful to have some time alone, she gave in to fatigue and crawled onto her cot by the far wall. Dusk was setting, the hot sun melting in the sky, gray streaks of night darkening the room. She closed her eyes, pulled the thin sheet over her legs and turned on her side. But a hollow emptiness settled inside her. She had felt it the moment she'd awakened in the shelter, freezing and delirious. She'd known then that she'd lost something. Something precious.

A loved one maybe.

Tears trickled down her cheek, but she angrily wiped them away. Remembering what had happened could help her return home. But what if she was right?

What if she'd blocked out the memory because someone she loved had died and she couldn't bear it?

Finally, exhaustion claimed her, but the nightmares returned to dog her, dragging her under a rushing wave of darkness, smothering and terrifying.

Someone was chasing her across the unforgiving land, toward the deep pockets and boulders. She tried to run but her legs felt heavy, her body weighted, and she skidded on the embankment, rocks tumbling downward and pinging off the canyon below. She tumbled and rolled, the sharp edges of the stones jabbing her skin and scraping her flesh raw.

Then his hands were on her, fingernails piercing as they bit into her shoulders. She fought back, swinging her hands up to deflect his blow, but he hit her so hard her head snapped back and stars danced in front of her eyes. Another blow followed, slamming into her skull and pain knifed behind her eyes, her breath gushing out as she tasted blood. She tried desperately to focus, to crawl away, but he yanked her by the ankles and dragged her across the rugged ground, the stones and bristly shrubs tearing at her hands and knees and face as she struggled to grasp something to hold on to.

God help her—he was going to kill her….

Somewhere close by, the river roared, water slashing over jagged rocks, icy cold water that would viciously suck her under and carry her away from everyone she loved.

No, she had to fight.

But the hands were on her again, this time around her throat, punishing fingers digging into her skin, gripping, squeezing, pressing into her larynx, cutting off her oxygen. She gulped and tried to fight back, swung her arms and kicked at him, but her body felt like putty, limp and helpless, as the world swirled into darkness.

Her heart pounding with terror, she jerked awake, disoriented and trembling. She'd only been dreaming; it had been the nightmares again….

She was safe.

But as she exhaled and her breathing steadied, a deadly stillness engulfed the pitch-dark room, the kind of eerie quiet before a storm that sent a frisson of alarm through her.

Then a breath broke the quiet.

A wheezing, whispery low sound. Someone was in the room.

Praying it was one of the sisters coming to check on her, she clenched the sheets and glanced across the space. The tall silhouette of a man stood in front of the open window in the shadows, the scent of sweat and cigarette smoke rolling off of him in sickening waves.

Pure panic ripped through her. Was it the man who'd tried to kill her in her dreams? One of the male abusers the women in the shelter were running from?

His hand moved to his waistband and the shiny glint of metal caught her eye.

She froze, body humming with adrenaline-spiked fear. A knife was tucked into the leather pouch attached to his belt.

She had to run.

Slowly she slid off the bed to escape and yelled for help, but he moved at lightning speed and trapped her. His big hands covered her mouth to silence her screams. She bit his hand, then clawed at him and cried out, fighting with all her might to throw his weight off of her.

Suddenly hall lights flickered on and footsteps clattered toward the doorway, doors banging open. The man's gaze shot sideways and he cursed, then lurched up, ran to the window and jumped out.

The sisters and three other women poured into the room, baseball bats in their hands, ready to attack.

The light flew on, throwing the room into a bright glare that nearly blinded her. Sister Margaret rushed to her, pulled her into her arms and soothed her. "He's gone now. You're safe, child."

It took her precious seconds to stop trembling, then anger ballooned inside her. She was tired of running, of hiding, of not knowing. They'd all assumed that whoever had hurt her had been a violent boyfriend or husband she'd been running from.

But she couldn't go on living like this. She had to know the truth. If her attacker was a boyfriend or husband, he'd found her. And she refused to be a coward.

Somewhere she had a life she'd left behind. And she wanted it back. Wanted the man who'd hurt her to pay.

And the person she'd lost—she had to face that truth, too.

"We should call the police," she whispered. "Send them my picture, Sister. I want to find out who I am and who's trying to kill me."

ONCE THE IDEA that Jack might possibly be his son entered Dylan's mind, he couldn't let it go. The baby shifted against him, finally falling back asleep, but Dylan didn't want to put him down. If the child was his, he wanted to know.

Dammit, he deserved to know.

Memories of his father taking him camping and fishing rolled back, and he saw himself doing the same thing with his own son one day.

When he'd first heard Aspen's baby had been found in her abandoned car, he'd assumed she'd moved on with her life, that she'd forgotten him, and had become involved with another man, someone on the reservation.

Because they'd been careful. And he'd trusted Aspen, trusted that she would have told him if she'd gotten pregnant with his baby.

But looking at Jack's big blue eyes now, he didn't know what to believe.

He settled into the rocking chair while Miguel made Emma herbal tea. Color returned to her cheeks as she sipped the hot brew, although distress still lined her face and her hand trembled slightly as she set the teacup back onto the saucer.

"Emma," he said quietly. "I have to ask you something, and I want you to be honest."

Her gaze met his, and she nodded, although she fidgeted with the afghan Miguel had draped around her shoulders. "I told you all I saw."

"It's not that," he said gruffly.

Her eyes softened as she watched the baby, indicating how much she loved her nephew.

"Emma, who is Jack's father?"

Emma bit down on her bottom lip and glanced away.

"The truth," he said, knowing if Aspen had confided in anyone it would have been her cousin. When Emma was a teenager, her mother's abusive boyfriend had set fire to the house, killing himself and Emma's mother. Emma had moved in with Aspen and her mother, Rose. After that, the girls had been more like sisters than cousins.

"I don't know," she said in a low voice. "Aspen never told me."

He arched a brow, a muscle ticking in his jaw. "Are you sure? You're not keeping some secret?"

Miguel squared his shoulders and draped a protective arm around Emma. "If she says she doesn't know, she doesn't."

"It's important," Dylan said, his throat thick. "Was she dating someone?"

Emma frowned. "Kurt Lightfoot, a builder from the reservation, was interested in her. They went out a few times. But… I'm not sure he fathered the baby." She hesitated. "He certainly hasn't claimed paternal rights."

"Where are you going with this?" Miguel asked. "Are you thinking that Jack's father might have been the one who attacked Aspen? That it wasn't like we suspected, that Boyd Perkins and Sherman Watts tried to kill her because she saw them dump Julie's body?"

Dylan hissed between clenched teeth. "I'm just considering every angle. And knowing Jack's father is important."

"Why is it so important to you?" Emma asked with odd twitch of her lips that made him wonder if she had a sixth sense about this, too.

He traced a finger over Jack's cheek, then decided that Emma might confide more if he came clean. "Because I might be the father."

Surprise flickered in Miguel's eyes, although Emma gave him a sympathetic look. "I honestly don't know," she said gently. "Aspen simply said that the baby's father wasn't in the picture. I assumed that he didn't want to be and didn't push her on the subject. It seemed to upset her too much."

Dylan's jaw snapped tight with the effort not to defend himself. He would have wanted to be in the picture. And if he discovered Jack was his, Aspen wouldn't get rid of him, either. Above all things, Dylan valued family and believed in a father's duty to take care of his children.

"You and Aspen?" Miguel asked.

Dylan gave a clipped nod. "The timing is right. We met in Vegas when I'd just come off that serial-killer case." God, the images of the dead Ute girls Frank Turnbull had killed still haunted him.

"Aunt Rose had just died then," Emma said quietly.

Dylan nodded. "I guess we both needed someone."

And he needed Aspen now and so did her baby… Possibly *their* baby.

Dammit, where was she?

Emma said she was in danger. Had Perkins or Watts found her?

Another possibility, one they hadn't considered, nagged at him.

If he wasn't the father, who was? Jack had been in that car when Aspen had crashed. He could have died, too.

If another man had fathered the little boy, had he tried to kill Aspen to keep his paternity a secret?

Chapter Two

Dylan's cell phone cut into the tense silence in the room, jarring Jack from sleep. He whimpered, and Dylan reluctantly handed him to Emma and connected the call.

"Acevedo speaking."

"Dylan, it's Tom Ryan. Listen, we just caught a break."

Dylan's pulse pounded. "What?"

"I'm at the Bureau now, and we received a fax from a women's shelter in Mexican Hat. It looks like we've found Aspen Meadows."

The blood roared through Dylan's veins. Trembling with relief, he muttered a silent prayer of thanks and crossed himself. "Is she all right?"

"She's alive. According to the sister I spoke with, she was brought in with injuries and has been healing there."

Fear gripped him again. "What kind of injuries?"

"I'm not sure. We didn't go into it. But I thought you might want to go to Mexican Hat and talk to her."

"Thanks. I will." In a brief moment of emotion, he'd confided in Tom that he had been involved with Aspen, that finding her was personal.

"I need to call Emma and tell her that we found her cousin."

"I'm with Emma and Miguel right now," Dylan said. "I'll let her know, then I'm on my way to Mexican Hat."

He disconnected the call, and turned to see Emma and his brother waiting with anticipation.

"They found Aspen?" Emma asked.

He nodded. "She's at a women's shelter in Mexican Hat."

"Thank God." Emma sagged in relief, although a second later, her nose wrinkled in confusion as she rocked Jack. "But if she's alive, why hasn't she called any of us? Why didn't she come back for Jack? She loved this baby more than anything in the world."

Dylan gritted his teeth. "I don't know. Only Aspen can tell us that. I'm going to bring her home."

"You want me to go with you?" Miguel asked.

Dylan shook his head and glanced at the baby. "No. Take a DNA swab from Jack and send it to the lab. And stick close to Jack and Emma. If Aspen is still in danger, her son might be, too."

Miguel agreed and Dylan rushed to the door, then outside to his sedan, worry knotting his stomach. Had Aspen been injured so badly she couldn't contact Emma? Had she been trying to protect her son by not returning?

He started the engine and raced away from Emma's house on the outskirts of Kenner City, anxious for answers.

If Jack was his son, he wanted to know why in the hell she hadn't trusted him with the truth. Not that he'd tried to contact her….

The little boy's baby blue eyes flashed into his head, and he grimaced. Jack had to be his—he knew it in his gut.

But as that possibility sank in, guilt assailed him.

If he'd been with Aspen and the baby, he could have protected them.

"ACCORDING TO THE FBI AGENT who phoned, your name is Aspen Meadows," Sister Margaret said.

Aspen clenched her hands together, weighing the name on her tongue. "Aspen..." Yes, that sounded right. Familiar.

Yet a sense of dread filled her as she waited for more information. "What else did he tell you?"

Sister Margaret stroked her arms to soothe her. "Just that your car was found crashed near the San Juan River, and that you've been missing for nine weeks. He's sending an agent here to talk to you and take you back to your family."

"Family?" Aspen jerked her head up, tears blurring her eyes. "I have family?"

Sister Margaret nodded with a smile. "I'm sure they've been worried sick about you. But don't fret now, child. You're finally going home."

Aspen bit down on her lower lip, more questions assailing her. If she had family, why didn't she remember them? And if she'd been running from an abusive boyfriend or husband, why hadn't she turned to her family for help?

A half-dozen scenarios raced through her head, fear gripping her. Maybe her family hadn't been loving at all. Maybe someone in that family had abused her.

Something about the scenario felt all too real...a distant memory plucking at her subconscious? Or had her contact with the women in the shelter stirred her imagination?

Since she'd arrived, she'd heard horror stories of wife and child beaters, fathers who'd sexually molested their daughters, of stalkers and possessive men who threatened and intimidated the very people they professed to care about, men who treated their women like property.

Had she left her family to protect them from the man after her?

Twice she'd seen a tall Ute man lurking outside, lingering near the fence surrounding the shelter. A Ute man who'd watched her and the other women with intense gray eyes that chilled her to the bone....

Was he the man who'd sneaked into her room and attacked her? Had she known him before?

And if he wanted her dead, would this FBI agent be able to protect her?

DYLAN'S EMOTIONS pinged between hopeful anticipation and trepidation over what he might find when he saw Aspen. He couldn't imagine the woman he knew deserting her child or not contacting her cousin to assure her she was safe.

Which meant her injuries must have been serious.

That or she was too scared to call home. And if that was the case, what had changed her mind?

The landscape swept by him with its pieces of flatland mingled with red-and-gray rocks, some twisted into convoluted shapes that as children, he and Miguel had played a guessing game to name when their family had driven through Colorado and Utah on family vacations. His mother had stopped to photograph the children playing outside their Navajo Indian houses. They'd camped along the San Juan and Colorado Rivers, visited Goosenecks State Park with its view of the steep cliffs and terraces, parked along the overhang and watched rafters take the long boat trip to Lake Powell.

God, they'd had so much fun during those trips. Muley Point had offered another view south over the twisting entrenched canyon to the desert beyond, and Monument Valley and the Valley of the Gods had been other favorite stops.

Baby Jack's face flashed into his mind and he wondered if he'd ever get to take his son camping along the ridges. If he'd be able to drive through the eerie formations of the Valley of the Gods and watch Jack's reaction when he first saw the sixty-foot-wide sombrero-shape rock that had inspired Mexican Hat's name.

He scrubbed his hand over the back of his neck—jeez, he was already thinking like Jack was his. Hoping he was....

If so, he had to find a way to make sure he stayed in the boy's life. Nothing Aspen could say would deter him.

U.S. 163 led him straight into town, and he let his GPS guide him down a side road to the shelter, a nondescript adobe building surrounded by a ten-foot iron gate. Inside, a massive cross stood in front of the steel door as if to guard its residents and stave off evil.

Dust and a wave of heat engulfed him as he climbed from his sedan, the gray night sky casting the center in dark shadows. He glanced around the outside but saw nothing amiss, so rang the buzzer at the gate entrance.

A second later, a woman's voice echoed through the speaker. "Yes?"

He produced his badge, then identified himself.

"Special Agent Ryan spoke with you about the photo you faxed to the Bureau, about the woman you have staying here. Aspen Meadows."

"Yes, just a minute." A buzz sounded, and the gate swung open, a nun appearing in the doorway to the building. She checked his identification before letting him enter, then led him to a small office to the right.

"I need to see her," he said without preamble.

Her eyes seemed to be assessing him. "First, we need to talk. My name is Sister Margaret."

He gave a clipped nod, noting the modest furnishings, a battered wooden desk and desk chair, two wooden Windsor chairs and a ratty plaid sofa that had seen better days. She gestured for him to take a seat, so he claimed one of the Windsor chairs, and she settled onto the sofa. But the pinched look on her face and the way she fidgeted with her habit spoke volumes about her mental state.

His gut churned with anxiety. "Is something wrong, Sister? Is Aspen all right?"

She pursed her lips and sighed, a sound that disturbed him even more.

"Did you personally know Aspen?" Sister Margaret asked.

He was accustomed to asking the questions. But this woman was as protective as a mother hen, so he knew he had to answer. "Yes. A while back. I've been investigating her disappearance for weeks. Her cousin is worried sick about her."

"Yes, about that..."

Dylan leaned forward, bracing his elbows on his knees. "Just cut to it, Sister. Is Aspen all right?"

"Yes, and no," the sister said. "When she first came to us, she was suffering from hypothermia, and multiple bruises and lacerations covered her body and face. Along with that, she had a couple of broken ribs, a fractured wrist, concussion and it appeared as if someone had tried to strangle her." She shuddered, and Dylan's mind raced with the visual image she'd painted.

"Can you tell me what happened to her?" Sister Margaret asked. "Who hurt her?"

Sweat beaded on Dylan's neck, and he took a deep breath, struggling to control his anger. "We don't have all the pieces of the puzzle yet. We believe she may have witnessed a murder. Either that or she saw the killer dumping a woman's body. When the killer realized Aspen had witnessed his criminal actions, he came after her. We found her car crashed along the San Juan River. Her son was inside."

"Oh, my." A horror stricken look passed over Sister Margaret's face. "Aspen has a son?"

"Yes, a baby boy named Jack. He's fifteen weeks old now." *And he might be mine.*

Sister Margaret pressed a hand to her pale face. "We thought she might be running from an abusive boyfriend or husband, but she never mentioned a child, so we had no idea. If we had, we would have reported her missing right away."

Dylan arched a brow, confusion clogging his head. "I don't understand. Didn't Aspen tell you what happened?"

"That's the reason I wanted to talk to you," Sister Margaret said softly. "Aspen was unconscious when she was brought in. And when she regained consciousness... well, she didn't remember anything."

Dylan's chest pounded. "You mean, she didn't remember the car crash or attack?"

Sister Margaret shook her head sadly. "I mean, she didn't remember *anything.* Not about what happened to her, not even her name or that she has family."

Dylan sat back in the chair, trying to absorb the missing piece the woman had just revealed. Amnesia would explain why Aspen hadn't contacted Emma or returned home for Jack.

Or called him for help.

"What did the doctor say about the amnesia?"

Sister Margaret looked shaken. "That the head injury could have caused her memory loss, but that the trauma could have been a factor, as well."

"Basically, she blocked out the events because they were too painful," Dylan said.

"Yes."

"Will she regain her memory?" Dylan asked.

The sister shrugged, her hands twisting together in her habit. "Probably. But that may take time. And Dr. Bennigan advised us not to push her, that doing so might traumatize her even more."

Dylan stewed over that revelation, bracing himself to meet an Aspen who had no idea who he was. "So what prompted you to finally report her appearance to the police?" Dylan finally asked.

The sister shifted nervously. "Someone broke into the center earlier, into the room where Aspen was sleeping and attacked her. She told us to call the police."

Dylan fisted his hands by his sides. Dammit, had Perkins and Watts tracked down Aspen and broken into the shelter to finish the job?

ASPEN SAT ON THE FLOOR with the children surrounding her, her voice low as she recanted the legend of the Sky People. "Manitou is the Great Spirit—he lived all alone in the sky. But he was lonely so he made a big hole in the sky and built the mountains, then sent snow and rain down to make the world more beautiful."

"Did he make the animals, too?" a curly red-haired four-year-old asked.

"Yes," Aspen said with a smile. "He made all the animals and the birds. But soon, like children and grown-ups do sometimes, the animals began to fight. So Manitou decided he needed a king to rule them all."

"Was it a lion?" a little boy asked.

"A dinosaur?" another suggested.

Aspen shook her head. "No, a grizzly bear." She reached up her arms and held them wide. "Now give me a big bear hug and say night-night."

The kids giggled and hugged her, and as they parted, she looked up to see Sister Margaret standing with a man in the doorway.

Her breath lodged in her chest in a painful surge. He was broad-shouldered and tall, so masculine with his wide jaw and chiseled features that her stomach fluttered with nerves. Thick black hair brushed his ears and forehead, long black lashes framing the bluest eyes she'd ever seen, eyes like the sky on a clear Colorado day.

Yet he looked dangerous and imposing, anger radiating off him in waves. And those startling eyes were intense, haunted, seemed to be trying to see deep into her soul, and made a chill skitter up her arms.

So did the scar that slashed his chin.

Although even that scar didn't detract from his good looks.

One of the mothers herded the children to the back rooms for bed, and Aspen stood slowly, her ankle still slightly weak from her tumble with her attacker.

Sister Margaret offered her a tentative smile and gestured for the man to follow.

"This is Special Agent Dylan Avecedo. He came to take you home, Aspen."

Fear slithered through Aspen as she met his gaze. Then he extended his hand and she placed hers inside his large palm, and a warm feeling of awareness shot through her. Something about those eyes seemed… familiar.

Had she met this man before?

But how would she have known a federal agent? Did he have the answers to her missing past?

And if he did, was she ready to hear the truth?

Chapter Three

God, Aspen was even more beautiful that he'd remembered. Seeing her sitting on the floor with those kids triggered childhood memories of his mother doing the same with him and his siblings.

And served as a reminder that Aspen had intended to help children before her life had been interrupted by a murder.

Her long dark hair hung in a thick braid over her shoulder, her chocolate colored eyes huge and so sultry that once again he lost himself in the beautiful depths.

They were also pensive, pained by her loss.

Damn, he could almost feel the turmoil inside her, the need to replace her missing past with the truth. Yet she instinctively knew the truth wouldn't be pretty, and she was frightened.

"Detective?" Her voice was pleading, searching his for answers. Answers that he didn't have.

He studied her for any sign of recognition, for any glimmer that she would welcome him back in her life. That she knew that he could be trusted to stay by her side.

But he saw no indication that she knew who he

was…or that she'd ever melted beneath his hands and mouth like a wanton lover.

Instead she looked at him as if he was a perfect stranger.

That hurt. He wanted her to know him, to recall what they'd had together, to want his touch as much as he craved hers.

Her face flushed slightly as he clung to her hand, and the trembling in her petite body and flushed expression in her eyes offered him a seed of hope. Even if she didn't remember him, there was something there, a simmering, immediate attraction, just as the first time they'd touched and fallen into bed.

She was serving cocktails in that casino in Vegas, wearing a short little black skirt with a cropped T-shirt that hugged her breasts and exposed the smooth brown flesh of her flat stomach. Her voice had purred like a kitten, her movements fluid and seductive, her body so tempting that he had had to caress her bare skin.

That body he knew so well. One he'd tasted and explored and memorized.

One he'd wanted so often over the past few months that he'd fantasized about having her again and again.

Somewhere in the building, a baby cried out, and he thought of Jack. Along with relief that she was physically okay and the instantaneous heat that ripped through him at the sight of her, anger churned through his gut.

Dammit, if Jack was his, why hadn't she told him?

Finally, she retreated and pulled away, wiping her palm on the side of her skirt. "Sister Margaret said you know where my family is."

A slight tremor laced her voice, and he tried to place himself in her shoes, to understand what it must be like to be lost and alone with no memory of what had happened, but obviously aware she was in danger.

"Yes, your cousin Emma is waiting at the Ute reservation. That's where you live. She's been searching for you ever since you disappeared."

A frown creased the delicate skin above her huge almond-shaped eyes. "How could I forget my own cousin?"

The doctor's advice trilled in his head like a warning bell, and Dylan forced an understanding smile. "You suffered a head injury," he said, hating the distress lining her face. "Sister Margaret said in time you may remember everything."

She shivered and wrapped her arms around her waist.

"Sister Margaret also said a man broke into your room. Did you get a look at your attacker?"

She shook her head. "No, it was too dark. All I saw was his shadow. Then he attacked me, and I fought back and screamed." Her voice broke, her breathing rattling out as if she was reliving that horrible event. "Then the sisters and other women ran in, and he jumped out the window and got away."

A fresh bruise darkened her cheek, and he gritted his teeth to keep from touching it and pulling her into his arms to comfort her. She looked so small and fragile and…vulnerable. "What else do you remember?"

She chewed her bottom lip. "He had a knife in a leather pouch attached to his belt."

Dylan's blood ran cold. "How tall was he?"

She hesitated, rubbing her head in thought. "I don't know. It was just a shadow."

"Did you notice a distinctive smell?"

"Cigarettes," she whispered. "And sweat."

Watts used to smoke but had supposedly given up the habit. But perhaps the man had picked it back up. "Did he say anything?"

She shook her head. "No, he just grabbed me and shoved his hand over my mouth. Then I…I think I bit his hand."

Her feistiness might have saved her life. Twice now. "I'd like to look around that room and see if I find any evidence."

Sister Margaret nodded, and he went to the sedan to retrieve his crime kit. He flipped on a flashlight, waving it across the room in an arc as he searched the corners, the bed and floor.

With a grunt, he knelt and with his gloved hand, retrieved a loose hair that had fallen on the floor. It might belong to one of the other women or children, but he'd check it out. The hair was longer than Boyd Perkins's or Sherman Watts's—but still, it might be a lead if there was a third perp.

Continuing the search, he paused at the window, then used a pair of tweezers to pluck a small piece of fabric that had caught on a nail on the windowsill, and bagged it along with the hair to send for analysis.

Maybe forensics would turn up something to help them nail the bastard and make sure the charges stuck when they finally tracked him down.

Stewing over the circumstances, he carried the evidence bags to the car while Aspen said goodbye to the other women. Outside, he phoned Miguel to explain the situation.

"Amnesia?" Miguel asked.

"Yes. She didn't recognize me. I'm hoping that seeing Emma and Jack will jog her memory."

"I'll warn Emma about the doctor's diagnosis," Miguel said. "And tell her not to push, to give Aspen time."

Five minutes later, Aspen returned carrying a small paper bag holding the meager possessions she'd accumulated since staying at the shelter.

Sister Margaret gave him a concerned look as she escorted them to the gate. "Take care of her, Agent Avecedo."

He squeezed her hand with a nod. "Don't worry. I won't leave her alone until we find out who hurt her." He paused and lowered his voice. "And, Sister, I'm going to need the medical report from when Aspen was brought in. When we find out who did this, it will help with prosecution."

If he let the son of a bitch live that long.

"I'll speak to the doctor, but we'll need a release from Aspen."

"I'll talk to her about it," Dylan said.

Sister Margaret agreed, then thanked him, and he walked Aspen to the car. She settled into the passenger side and buckled her seat belt, the tension thickening as he drove away from the shelter.

"Sister Margaret said that you were injured when you arrived at the center. That you thought that someone, an abusive boyfriend, was after you."

She shrugged. "It seemed like a likely story, Agent Acevedo."

"Call me Dylan."

She gave him an odd look, then nodded.

"Did the abusive boyfriend idea come from a memory?" he asked.

She fidgeted, looking back at the center as if she wanted to return to the safe haven she'd found within that iron fence. "Not really. Just a feeling that I was running from someone." Her voice warbled. "And then there are the nightmares."

"Nightmares?"

She nodded, her brown eyes huge in her face. "Nightmares of fighting some man, of running, of hearing the river and being cold…"

She angled her head to study his face. "Can you fill in any of the missing pieces?"

"Some, but not all. We found your car smashed into a tree by the San Juan River." He paused, debating over whether to tell her that her son had been left in her car. "There was evidence of a struggle. Blood in the car. We didn't know if you'd survived or if you might have drowned in the river."

She made a low sound in her throat. "My cousin… She was worried?"

He nodded and gently placed his hand over hers in an attempt to calm her, although heat radiated through him. He wanted more, wanted to hold her and assure her everything would be all right.

Wanted to shake her for not telling him that they had a son together.

"Yes, Aspen, her name is Emma, and she's anxious for you to come home."

Relief filled her eyes, and she relaxed slightly. As much as he wanted to press her, he forced himself to rein in his emotions and let her absorb what he'd told her.

"You look exhausted," he said. "Why don't you try

to rest during the drive? I know Emma will want to talk when we arrive."

She gave him a wary look, but nodded. A second later, she curled up against the door and fell asleep, but even in sleep, her body seemed wound tight and braced for battle as if she expected her attacker to reappear any minute and end her life as he'd tried to do before.

THE NIGHTMARES RETURNED AGAIN.

Aspen struggled to wake herself, determined not to let them suck her into the darkness, but the heavy pull of fear yanked her back to the day she'd been running.

Running, but from whom?

If she could only see the man's face…

She crawled along the steep rocks, fighting to steady herself as the river raged below, the snow-capped ridges reminding her that the water would be dangerous and freezing. That although she was an excellent swimmer, there was no way she could survive the icy temperatures or strong current.

Then the hands were upon her, clenching, hitting, choking her, dragging her into the murky depths of death.

She screamed, snippets of her life flashing in front of her. The Ute reservation, the casino, the Trading Post, the children gathering for a Ute celebration. The Bear Dance in the spring and the Sun Dance at Mesa Verde.

Her mother teaching her the ways of the people. The childhood stories of the Sky People, the legend of the Sleeping Ute Mountain, and the ghost stories her mother insisted she pass on about the sacrifices of their ancestors.

Then she was drowning, the icy water sucking her

down to the bottom, the rocks beating against her skin, the whisper of death calling her name.

She jerked awake, shaking and disoriented. Suddenly she felt the agent's hand on hers again. "More nightmares, Aspen?"

She lifted her head, pushed a strand of hair that had escaped her braid from her eyes and tried to steady her labored breathing. "Yes." She glanced down at his hand, aching to cling to him for protection, but she hardly knew the man. Still, he made her feel safe as if he wouldn't leave her to the terrifying memories that hacked at her sanity, tapping at the fringes of her conscience yet evading her.

While she'd slept, the weather had changed. Dark ominous clouds hovered above the ridges, the mountain runoff filling the potholes and shoulder with rising water. A chill filled the car, the temperatures dropping as they neared the canyon.

The road was virtually deserted, the landscape colored with shadows, prairie grass and scattered rocks. In the distance, the sound of a coyote rent the air, the slap of the windshield wipers battling the light rain eerie in the silence.

Occasionally they passed a pueblo style house, the elements having beaten its beauty to a muddy brownish orange. The story she'd told the children earlier reminded her that this area was dangerous territory for the reemergence of the grizzly bear.

And the ghost town that had once been a miner's haven made her anxious to return to civilization.

A gust of wind that sounded like a freight train sent tumbleweed swirling across the road, then suddenly bright headlights appeared behind them, racing up on their tail.

Aspen tensed as Dylan swerved, the car bounced over a rut in the road and hit a wet patch. The car behind them rammed into their tail, sending the sedan fishtailing across the dark highway, skimming rocks and spewing gravel and dirt.

Dylan cursed in Spanish and steered into the skid in an attempt to regain control.

But the car raced up behind them, rammed them again, then swerved to their right and a gunshot pierced the side of the car.

Aspen screamed, and Dylan shoved her head down. "Stay low!"

Dylan sped up, weaving left then right, as if he intended to outsmart their attacker at his own game of cat and mouse. The sedan sent the other car sliding off the road toward the creek, which looked as if it was about to flood from the mountain runoff.

Aspen covered her head with her hands, leaning down so her forehead touched her knees. But a second later, the other car's tires squealed and the vehicle slammed into them again. Another shot shattered the window on the passenger side, sending glass raining down on top of her.

She cried out again, and Dylan shouted another obscenity, losing control as the sedan careened off the road, bounced over shrubs and rocks and hit a tall rock formation. Metal screeched and gears ground together as they spun toward the ridge out of control. The car flipped on its side, rolled and landed upside down in the creek bed. The air bag exploded, knocking the wind out of her and trapping her in the seat.

Aspen thought she might have passed out for a moment, and when she recovered, her breath huffed out in tiny pants as water began to seep through the window.

"Are you okay?" Dylan shouted.

They were both hanging upside down, the seat belt cutting into her neck. She glanced sideways and noticed blood dotting his hands, and felt it trickling down her arm where glass had pelted them.

"Aspen?"

"Yes, I'm okay," she rasped. "But water's coming in."

"I know. Hang on to the seat belt and side of the car while I cut you out."

She sucked in a sharp breath and braced herself with one hand on the roof of the car and another on the door. Dylan retrieved a knife from his pocket and sawed at her air bag, puncturing it. It deflated with a whoosh, then he sawed at her seat belt. The icy water gurgled and spewed through the window, dripping onto the roof and soaking her.

"Hurry!" she whispered hoarsely as déjà vu struck her. She'd been in another crash and had almost drowned....

Her dreams of running, of being cold—they weren't just nightmares. They had been very real.

"Almost got it," Dylan said between clenched teeth.

The belt finally snapped, and she slid downward, her head hitting the roof. "Try to climb out," he said. "I need to cut my belt."

Terror seized her. She didn't want to go out there alone.

"Go, Aspen!"

His sharp voice jerked her from the fear gripping her, and she maneuvered sideways, then kicked the rest of the glass free with her feet. Water gushed inside the vehicle, and she held her breath, grabbed the seat and shoved her weight through the window. The freezing water swallowed her, and numbness claimed her, but her foot connected with rock, and she used it as a springboard to propel her. Teeth chattering, she waded to the embankment.

Dragging in huge gulping breaths, her limbs shaking, she searched the creek and finally saw Dylan wading toward her in the waist-deep cold water.

He crawled from the creek, carrying the crime-scene kit in one hand. Another gunshot blasted the rock beside her, and Dylan grabbed her hand. "Come on, let's go!"

Her legs felt like Jell-O as he yanked her to her feet and dragged her across the embankment. She stumbled over rocks, and her ankle twisted but she plunged on, ducking low to dodge another bullet.

She couldn't die now, not when she'd just found out her name, and that she had family waiting for her.

Chapter Four

Dylan stuffed the evidence box beneath a boulder, then buried Aspen in the crook of his arm to protect her from the gunshots as they raced in an upward climb into the mountains. The terrain was rocky and pitted with shrubs and brush, the jagged ridges posing their own danger.

It was also a good place to hide.

Another shot pinged off a stone jutting out from the ridge, and they ducked, dodging it as he pushed her behind a boulder. The dark sky and mixture of rain and snow added to the dangers, making their footing slippery. A second later, he steered her toward another indentation carved into the red stone, pushing her to climb higher as they dodged more bullets.

Dylan crouched beside her, removed his gun and braced it to fire. "Stay down," he whispered. "I'm going after the bastard."

She grabbed his arm. "No. Don't leave me alone."

The cold terror in her voice and eyes made his chest clench, and he hated the shooter for putting it there. All the more reason to catch the SOB.

He brushed his hand against her bruised cheek. "I'll be back."

Slowly rising behind the boulder, he searched the ridges and cliffs, then spotted movement to the right. He fired, a shot pinging over the shadow, and rocks skittered down the ridge as the man scrambled to escape.

Dylan gestured for Aspen to stay put, then lurched forward in chase. He fired again and saw the shadow moving at lightning speed around a boulder, then disappear. Dylan wanted to pursue him, but a low cry escaped Aspen and a faraway look glazed her eyes as if she was reliving the trauma that had caused her amnesia.

Her arm was bleeding, too, and cuts from the shattered window marred her hands.

The sound of a car engine sliced the night, and Dylan breathed a sigh of relief, then stooped down and gathered Aspen in his arms. She trembled against him, wet and shivering, and he hugged her to his chest, whispering low words of assurance.

Thank God they had survived.

But he'd find the man who'd tried to kill him and put that terror in Aspen's eyes and make him suffer.

ASPEN CLUNG TO THE AGENT, memories of another crash and running for her life bombarding her. She survived, she reminded herself, and she would survive now.

At least this time she wasn't alone.

"It's all right, Aspen," Dylan said. "He's gone now and you're safe."

She forced a calming breath, then looked up at him. "But he'll be back. And how can I fight him if I don't even know who he is?"

"Sister Margaret said you would get your memory back," he assured her. "You need time. Just trust me for now."

She folded her arms. "It's just so frustrating and scary. I feel as if I'm living in the dark."

He stroked her back, soothing her. "I won't stop until the danger to you is over and the man responsible for the shooting and for your memory loss is in jail, or dead."

She took solace in his strength, relaxed slightly and pulled herself together.

He wiped the blood dotting her arm. "We need to take you to the E.R."

"No. I'm all right," she said. "It's just a few scratches." She pressed a finger to his forehead. "But you might need stitches."

He shrugged off her concern and slowly extracted himself from her arms. "I'm fine. But I need to call for help."

She nodded, then he removed his cell phone and made a call, thankful it still worked.

"Tom, it's Dylan. Listen, I was driving Aspen back to the reservation and someone ambushed us. My car is upside down in the creek and we need an extraction. Also, I want forensics to go over the car for paint samples and bullets." He gave him their location, disconnected the call, then turned to her and took her arm.

"Come on, let's head back down to the car. I need to retrieve the evidence box to send to forensics."

Aspen took his hand as he helped her down the slippery rocks, grateful the precipitation had stopped, although the wind rustled the brush and ruffled her damp hair. Her hands and feet were numb already, the chill inside her mounting. He paused to grab the crime scene kit with the evidence bags he'd stowed inside and hoisted it in one hand while keeping the other firmly on her arm to steady her.

By the time they reached the bottom, the sound of a helicopter echoed from above, its blinking lights sweeping the terrain and promising a recovery.

The helicopter touched down in the flatter part of the canyon and two men climbed out, the pilot and another big guy, an Indian, who frowned as he stalked toward them.

Dylan stepped forward. "Ryan didn't say he was sending you, Bia. But I'm glad he did." He gestured toward Aspen. "This is Aspen Meadows. Aspen, Special Agent Ethan Bia. He's an expert tracker with the Bureau."

The Indian nodded and glanced at Aspen. "Nice to meet you, Miss Meadows."

"Please, call me Aspen."

"Sure." He angled his head toward Dylan. "Ryan didn't know what we'd find, if the shooter was still hiding around here and you might be holed up in the mountains."

"I ran him off," Dylan said. "But we need to collect the bullet casings and take paint samples from my car. When we find this SOB, I want to make sure we have forensics to back up an arrest."

Ethan nodded. "Absolutely. I'll look for the bullet casings while the pilot flies you two back. Ryan's sending a team and a tow truck for the car. I'll wait on them and make sure CSI processes it."

"Thanks." Dylan shook his head, and curved an arm around Aspen, coaxing her toward the chopper. "Come on, let's get you warmed up and to the E.R."

Aspen had never ridden in a helicopter but she was

too cold and tired to argue, so she crawled in beside Dylan, accepted the blanket he offered and burrowed beneath it while the blades of the chopper whirled and they lifted off.

Her gaze fell to Dylan's car where it lay upside down in the rising creek, and she flinched. They could have died and they might not have been found for days or weeks.

The realization that that was the shooter's plan sent another shudder through her. She had to remember what had happened nine weeks ago.

Her life depended on it.

THE NEXT FEW HOURS were hectic and strained as the helicopter transported them to the emergency room in Durango, and doctors examined and treated them for scrapes and cuts. Dylan earned four stitches to his forehead, but thankfully Aspen didn't need stitches. Still, she was bruised and battered and had suffered minor lacerations on her hands and legs.

He phoned Miguel, explained the circumstances and suggested he take Aspen home to rest before she saw Jack. Miguel promised to leave a key to Aspen's house hidden in the mouth of the horse sculpture in her front yard.

Fatigue lined her face as he secured a vehicle, dropped the evidence he'd collected earlier at the Kenner County Crime Unit in Kenner City, and drove toward the reservation. It was early morning, the gray dawn sky filled with the shadows of another impending storm. Neither of them had slept for over twenty-four hours, and he desperately needed a shower and food.

"Where are we going?" Aspen asked.

Her labored breath as she pressed a hand to her

chest indicated her ribs were bruised from the impact of the air bag. If she felt like him, every bone in her body ached.

"To your house for some sleep. Then we'll reconnect with your family. Your cousin dropped off some groceries earlier if you're hungry."

"But, Dylan—"

"Don't argue, Aspen," he said, cutting her off. "You've had a lot to deal with in the past twenty-four hours and need some rest before you face your family."

And so did he. Because he wanted to be prepared when she saw Jack for the first time. "The doctor warned that you need to take it easy and not push things for your own health."

Wariness dimmed her features, but exhaustion and trauma outweighed any protest as her eyes slid closed. He clenched his jaw, hating the bruises on her battered skin and the fact that she'd forgotten everyone she loved. That fact alone confirmed the extent of physical and mental trauma she'd suffered.

And as much as he wanted to question her about Jack's paternity, he had to refrain.

Earn her trust. Give her time to heal. To reconnect with her family and home and let her memories return on their own.

Or he could drive the truth deeper into her psyche.

Which meant it would be even more difficult to find out who had attacked her.

And he had to do that to protect her.

If Boyd Perkins and Sherman Watts had tried to kill her, she'd have to testify so they could put the men behind bars.

Of course, they had to find the bastards first.

And if someone else was involved…well, he'd find that out and uncover their motive. If Jack wasn't his son and another man was in the picture…

No, he couldn't go there yet.

But he needed to brace himself for that possibility. Couldn't allow himself to get too close to her or the baby until he knew the truth.

Did she think he wasn't father material? Couldn't she contemplate a future with him?

Agitated, mind racing with questions, he drove onto the reservation toward Aspen's. He wasn't surprised at the small pueblo style house with its adobe colors and Native American look. During their one glorious week in Vegas together, she'd talked about life on the reservation, her love of her culture, and her desire to teach the children and instill in them the importance of their heritage.

Aspen was deep in sleep, so he parked in the stone drive, climbed out and grabbed the key, his instincts on full alert as he scanned the property.

Satisfied no one was hiding in the shadows of the trees, he left Aspen in the car while he went to search the inside. Darkness bathed the interior as he entered, and he paused to listen for sounds of an intruder.

First thing tomorrow, he'd install a security system in Aspen's home. One that went straight to him if anyone set off the alarm.

Slowly, he crept inside the dark entryway, flipped on a light, then scanned the foyer. Native American artwork decorated the adobe colored walls, collections of handmade baskets, beaded jewelry, pottery and other artifacts and books filled the built-in shelves. A picture of a native Ute on horseback was centered over a soft brown leather couch opposite a woodstove in the den, which opened to the kitchen.

He moved to the left and found a master suite and bath, decorated in earth tones with accents of red, yellow and orange, and more Ute art. He searched the closet, beneath the bed, then moved to the guest bedroom on the opposite side of the kitchen.

His lungs tightened at the sight of the nursery. A primitive wooden crib sat in the midst of the freshly painted baby blue room, which held an assortment of stuffed animals, children's books and infant toys.

Hissing a breath of relief that no intruder was inside, he stowed his gun inside his jacket, then went outside to the car and lifted Aspen from the seat. She moaned softly in her sleep, and snuggled against him as he carried her to the front stoop.

She was wrapped in the blanket, wearing the scrubs the nurse had given her at the E.R. when they'd removed her damp clothes, so he carried her to her bedroom, pulled down the covers and laid her on the crisp clean sheets. For a brief second her eyes flickered open, and she looked at him with glazed eyes.

He inhaled her sweet fragrance, the softness of her skin, and ached to crawl in bed beside her. To rekindle the heat between them.

"You're home now," he said gently, then pulled the quilt over her and brushed back her hair.

She tugged at his hand, and a hollow feeling of need gripped him.

"Where are you going?' she whispered in a sleep-laced voice that triggered images of the two of them in bed together, of her voice purring his name after a night of lovemaking.

"I know it sounds silly," she whispered, "but I don't want to be alone."

God, he didn't want that, either. He wanted to make love to her.

Instead, he brushed the pad of his thumb across her cheek. "I'll sleep on the couch," he said, his voice thick and hoarse. "If you need me just call."

She nodded, closed her eyes again and curled into her bed. He ached to drop a kiss on her cheek, then her mouth, but remembered the doctor's warning and forced himself to leave the room.

Still, his body hummed with arousal and a fierce hunger that could only be sated by Aspen.

A woman who saw him as a perfect stranger.

Chapter Five

Dylan was exhausted but on edge, too wired to sleep.

It was the first time he'd been in Aspen's home and he felt uncomfortable and intrigued at the same time. Her furnishings were exactly as he'd expected, reminiscent of her culture, yet the sight of the nursery made his chest ache.

How would she react when she saw the empty baby bed? When she saw Jack? Would she remember her son?

He yanked off his shirt and walked around the den/kitchen combination, wishing he was here under other circumstances. That Aspen had invited him into her home because she wanted to see him again.

He studied the Ute items in the room and was once again reminded of the road trips his family used to take when he was younger.

Once they'd stopped to observe a young Ute woman with a horde of children surrounding her as she taught them to weave baskets. His mother had photographed her, and he'd thought about that photograph when he'd first seen Aspen.

The Uncompahgre beaded horse bag on Aspen's wall was made from tanned mule deer hide. Thousands of glass trade beads and tobacco balls were stitched into the sides and rim. The bags were used to hold pipes, carvings and religious totems and were opened only for private ceremonies.

An Uncompahgre Ute Shaved Beaver Hide Painting hung above the fireplace, and ceremonial pipes of salmon alabaster and black pipestone sat on the mantle. Several ceremonial rattles made from buffalo rawhide that were used to call spirits in Ute ceremonies decorated a pine sofa table.

Some Ute still used peyote in healing rituals. He wondered if Aspen did, or if she would use a traditional doctor with their son.

Her *son—you don't know yet that Jack is yours.*

Still, his gaze was drawn to the photographs, and he walked over to study the scattering of pictures. The first photo showed Aspen cradling a newborn to her chest. Dylan touched the frame, memorizing the picture. The baby's eyes were squished closed, his lips pursed, his fists on his chest.

The next one had been taken a couple of weeks later. A smiling Jack was propped against a Mexican blanket. The scant few pictures chronicled his young life up until the time Aspen had disappeared.

Jack had only been four weeks old at the time.

Aspen had missed almost three months of her son's life because of the attack.

And if Jack was his, he had missed those months, as well.

Dammit, he would find out who'd stolen those weeks from her and make sure she and Jack were never separated again.

HOURS LATER, Aspen woke from an exhausted sleep to the delicious aroma of coffee. Still groggy, she rolled over in bed and looked at her surroundings. A fog still hovered over her memories, but the room, the art, the scent of lavender seemed familiar and evoked a warm fuzzy feeling as if she was finally safe.

Then the events of the night before crashed back, shattering her peace. Her limbs throbbed as she swung her legs over the side of the bed. A sharp pain splintered her midriff from her bruised ribs, and she breathed deeply to stem the pain, gripping the edge until her legs steadied enough to support her.

She was still wearing the scrubs the nurse had given her in the E.R., and desperately wanted a shower.

Footsteps in the den sounded, and she hesitated, the fear that had clawed at her the last few weeks returning. Who was in the house?

That agent—Dylan? Or someone else?

A tremor rattled the windowpane, and she stood and walked to the edge of the door and glanced into the den. Dylan Acevedo was sitting at the table, drinking coffee and looking at an opened folder.

Relief surged through her, and she hurried into the bathroom. The warm water felt heavenly on her achy body and helped to wash away the scent of the river and soothe her aching limbs. After toweling off, she let her hair hang loose to dry, and dug through the closet, noting the long flowing Indian skirts and beaded blouses. She chose a bright blue skirt, pale yellow blouse and a pair of leather sandals and dressed, then walked into the den.

Dylan glanced up, his dark blue eyes raking over her and sending a tingle through her.

But his mouth was set in a firm straight line, and the sultry look she thought she'd seen suddenly died, an iciness replacing it.

"I can't believe I slept so long." She accepted the mug of coffee he offered, surprised when he automatically dumped a packet of sweetener in it as if he knew how she liked it.

She started to question him about that, but he cleared his throat. "Your cousin Emma has already called. I told her we'd let her know when you woke up. She's anxious to see you."

Nerves fluttered in Aspen's stomach. "What if I don't recognize her?"

His dark look softened. "Don't worry. She knows about your amnesia."

A helpless feeling engulfed her. "But how could I forget my own family?"

He took her elbows in his hands, then guided her to the table. "You will remember. Just give yourself time to heal. Now why don't I make you something to eat and then we'll call Emma?"

She nodded and sipped her coffee as he made himself at home and whipped up two omelets. Odd that Dylan seemed comfortable in the kitchen—and in his skin.

When he placed the plates on the table, he set the hot sauce on the table. She immediately reached for it, something niggling at the back of her mind. How did he know she liked hot sauce on her eggs?

"Any more nightmares?" he asked as he sprinkled salt and pepper on his food.

She pressed a hand over her forehead, struggling with the tiny snippets of life that flashed in front of her. Another man cooking for her, feeding her in bed…

His big body taking up all the space in the room just as Dylan's was now.

"Aspen, are you all right? You're not eating."

She blinked to clear her head and cut into her omelet. "I think I was too exhausted to have nightmares. Either that or I felt…safe for the first time in weeks."

His breath rushed out and their gazes locked, the moment stretching between them before he finally broke the strained silence. "I'm glad you felt safe."

She frowned. Her comment seemed ridiculous—how could she feel safe when they'd been attacked and nearly died the night before?

Because Dylan was watching over her, protecting her, guarding her house. Deep down, she sensed he wouldn't let anyone hurt her.

He was an excellent agent, took his job seriously.

But there was more. He'd promised to protect her. And somehow, she knew that he kept his promises.

Still, nerves pulled at her sanity. And a voice whispered inside her head that she couldn't grow dependent on the agent. That she needed to keep her distance.

That hollow ache clutched her insides again. She'd never be whole again until she found out the truth.

Time for her to meet her cousin.

THE FACT THAT ASPEN FELT SAFE with him helped to dissipate his anger over the awkward situation.

A knock sounded at the door and he gestured to her that he'd get it. He checked the window and saw Miguel's vehicle, then heard the rumble of his brother talking to Emma through the door. His jaw tightened as he opened it and saw Jack cradled in Emma's arms.

"Come on in, Aspen is waiting."

When he glanced back at Aspen, she was standing in front of the mantle, studying the baby pictures, tears shimmering in her eyes.

Emma's expression lit with excitement, although nerves also shimmered in the depths of her eyes as Aspen turned to face her.

Miguel closed the door, and Dylan angled himself to watch the reunion, feeling touched, but out of place as if he was an outsider, an intruder in this family.

A family that should be his.

"Oh, Aspen…" Emma's voice choked as she walked over to her. "I've been out of my mind with worry."

Aspen raked her dark brown eyes over Emma and Jack. "Emma?"

"Yes, it's me. I'm so relieved to have you home." Emma gestured toward Jack, a loving expression softening the anxious lines on her face. "We've both missed you."

As if he understood, Jack whimpered, scrunching up his nose and Emma rocked him back and forth.

"My baby…" Aspen whispered.

Emma nodded. "Jack. They found him in your car after the accident."

Aspen paled, and Dylan hurried over and coaxed her to the sofa. "Take a deep breath," Dylan murmured.

She did as he said, then turned tortured eyes to him. "I abandoned my little boy?" Shock made her voice sound screechy. "I can't believe I'd do that. What kind of mother am I?"

"You were—are—a wonderful mother," Emma said firmly.

Dylan stroked her back. "You didn't leave him of your own accord."

"Then you know what happened to me?"

Dylan, Emma and Miguel exchanged a frustrated look, each questioning just how much to confess. "We know that someone ran you off the road and attacked you," Dylan said. "That was evident from the injuries you sustained and were treated for at the shelter."

"I knew I was missing something," she said in a heartbreakingly agonized voice. "Every time I hugged one of the kids at the center I knew it."

"You love Jack," Emma said gently. "You would never have left him willingly."

"Who did this to me?" Aspen asked, her tormented gaze lingering on her son.

"We're not sure," Dylan said. "Miguel and I are both on the team investigating your disappearance."

Aspen nodded weakly, then pressed her hands to her thighs as if to dry the dampness from them, then reached up toward Emma. "Can I hold him? Can I hold my baby?"

"Of course you can, Aspen," Emma said softly. She moved closer then settled down beside Aspen and jiggled Jack to quiet him.

Aspen's chin trembled and a tear slid down her cheek as she took the squirming baby into her arms. "You are mine, aren't you, Jack?" Aspen whispered. "My God, I've missed you." She hugged him to her and Jack immediately quieted, a little chirp coming from his mouth as he gazed up at his mother. Aspen brushed a hand across his thick, dark hair, then lowered a kiss to his cheek.

"I'm home now, son." She nuzzled his cheek with her own and Jack cooed, reached out his tiny fist and pulled a strand of her hair. Aspen laughed softly, then kissed his cheek. "I'm so sorry I left you, Jack. You must have been so scared..." She lifted him to her chest and hugged him tightly. "I promise I'll never leave you again."

A tenderness warmed Dylan's insides, as well as protective urges that nearly overpowered him.

But once again Aspen looked at him as if he was a stranger and a pang ripped through his heart. He was already coming to think of Jack—and Aspen—as his.

Which he couldn't allow himself to do.

There might have been another man in her life since they'd parted a year ago, another man who'd fathered her child.

But if there was, why hadn't he stepped up to take care of her and Jack?

And if there was, was he responsible for the attack on Aspen at the shelter, or had that been Perkins or Watts?

ASPEN'S HEART MELTED as she hugged her son to her. She finally felt whole again, as if she'd found the most important part of her missing life.

Yet frustration filled her as she studied her son's features and searched her memory banks for some semblance of details about his birth.

And the person who'd taken her away from him.

Dylan frowned, then asked Miguel to step outside, leaving her alone with Emma and the baby. Jack nestled against her shoulder, poked his thumb in his mouth and made sucking sounds.

"Are you really all right?" Emma asked.

"I will be," Aspen said, trying to sound convincing although questions swirled in her head.

Emma placed a comforting hand on her shoulder. "You know, I saw you," she said in a strained voice.

"What do you mean? Were you there at the accident?"

"No, not exactly." A shyness crept into Emma's blue eyes. "I forget that you have amnesia. I have psychic visions, Aspen. I saw you running from a man. I was terrified for you."

Aspen glanced down at Jack, who'd fallen asleep on her shoulder.

"Come on," Emma said, taking her elbow.

"Where are we going?"

"To put Jack back in his own bed."

Aspen followed her to the second bedroom, and a smile crept over her face at the sight of the nursery. For a brief moment, she saw an image of herself painting the room, of Emma helping her set up the changing table, of baby Jack watching the mobile twirl as it played a lullaby.

Another memory followed, this one of her and Emma playing together as children. Of Emma crying because a man had hurt her mother.

The memories blipped in and out of focus so quickly that she thought she might have imagined them. But they were so real, she knew they were truths pushing their way through the darkness that had consumed her the last few weeks. Those brief snippets gave her hope that she'd remember everything.

But the image of Emma crying disturbed her. Her father…no her mother's boyfriend had been abusive just as some of the women's husbands had been at the shelter.

She gently placed Jack inside the crib, then glanced at her left hand. She hadn't been wearing a ring on her finger when she'd been carried to the shelter. And there was no imprint indicating she'd ever had one.

She turned to Emma, debating over whether to ask, but she needed answers. The sisters had thought an abusive man might be after her. What if it was Jack's father?

"Emma, can I ask you something?"

"Of course, Aspen. Whatever you need."

Aspen tucked a yellow baby blanket over her son. "Who is Jack's father?"

Emma sighed softly and motioned for her to go to the den. After they settled on the sofa, Emma took her hand. "You didn't tell me, Aspen. All you said was that he wasn't in the picture."

"What about another friend? Is there someone else who I'd have told?"

"You're friends with Naomi Rainwater, another teacher on the reservation, but you told me that no one knew, and you intended to keep it that way."

Aspen frowned and glanced at the baby pictures on the mantle. Why wouldn't she have wanted anyone to know Jack's father?

Was he dangerous? Had she been running from him?

DYLAN ACEVEDO thought he would trap him. Thought he would keep the Indian girl and her kid safe by hovering over them.

But he was wrong.

Acevedo and the other pigs had treated him like dirt way too long. Had hunted him like a dog and would keep on hunting.

But he was the hunter now. He was watching their movements. Knew exactly where they were and what they were doing.

Because he was smarter than them all.

And the girl…killing her would serve his cause *and* torture Acevedo.

Pure pleasure bubbled in his chest as he flicked the cigarette butt to the ground outside Aspen's house and watched the embers spark to life on the brittle scrub grass, then slowly fade as the fire turned the blades a parched brown. He'd quit the cigarettes once, but his craving had returned.

No one knew he was here now or the reason why.

But they would soon.

Because the girl absolutely had to die.

A smile curved his lips.

In fact, he was looking forward to it.

Chapter Six

Dylan left Miguel to guard Aspen and Emma while he headed to the crime lab in Kenner City. But first he drove to Durango to his apartment to pack a bag to carry to Aspen's. He fully intended to stay with her until he was certain she was safe.

His mail had piled up, but he bypassed it and showered first, then packed his clothes and toiletries and stowed them in the rental car. His apartment seemed bare, quiet, empty. Lonely. As if no one lived there, not homey like Aspen's comfortable pueblo style house.

There was no baby here. No woman to love. No one to come home to or to care if he lived or died.

His chest ached, but he clamped a mental stronghold on his thoughts. He'd grown up in a loving home, but he'd gotten into some trouble as a teenager with a gang, but finally turned himself around. He'd told himself his job didn't fit with a wife and kid. That his work would put them in danger.

Although he'd stayed away, Aspen was still in danger.

And if he'd been around this last year, she might be safe now.

A brown manila envelope jutting out of the stack of mail caught his eye and he thumbed through the other pieces, then picked up the envelope with a frown. It was from Julie Grainger.

Ben Parrish and Tom Ryan had received packages from her with different medals inside. Ben had received the medal of St. Joan of Arc, the patron saint of captives, and seemed upset by the sight of it, Tom received a St. Christopher medal, the patron saint of travelers. Dylan wondered what his held and what the significance of each one meant.

Why had she sent each of them a gift? Had she known she was in trouble, that she might die?

Anxious to see if the contents led to a clue to the case, he ripped open the envelope and found a religious medal of Raphael the Archangel, the patron saint against nightmares.

He smiled at her choice.

Julie had known how much his sister's death and the Turnbull case had destroyed his nights. She'd tried to convince him to forgive himself, that he couldn't save them all, but dammit, he felt responsible.

His thumb brushed something else, and he dug deeper and found a photograph inside. An old black and white of a young Vincent Del Gardo and Belinda MacBride Douglas, Callie MacBride's mother.

What did the photo mean? That Del Gardo and Callie's mother had known each other years ago? That they'd been friends?

Or lovers?

Did Callie know they shared a past?

Hell, Del Gardo was a crime boss and their main

suspect in Julie Grainger's murder. They also believed that Boyd Perkins had killed Del Gardo, which had brought Del Gardo's rival crime organization, the Wayne family, into the limelight of the investigation, complicating matters more.

Dylan would take the medal and photo to the crime lab, show them to Callie and see what she said. Maybe it was a missing clue of some kind.

He hurried to the annex building housing the Kenner County Crime Unit, took the elevator to the third floor and decided to check with ballistics before he talked to Callie.

Jerry Griswold, the crime lab's firearms expert, was examining a bullet as he entered and had several more shell casings spread on the table.

"Are those from the shooter who fired at my car last night?"

Jerry nodded and gestured toward the screen indicating the National Integrated Ballistics Information Network. "Bia did good. Looks like the bullet casings came from a .38. I checked NIBIN but didn't find a match. If I had the weapon, I could compare and verify if it belongs to the shooter."

Dylan rubbed his chin, then caught himself as his fingers brushed his scar. Boyd Perkins had a nine millimeter. Of course, he could have a whole cache of weapons, for all they knew. "I'll do my best to find it," Dylan said.

He thanked Jerry, then headed to the other part of the lab. Callie, the head of forensics, glanced up from her microscope. "Hey, Acevedo."

"Hi, Callie. Have you had a chance to process the evidence from the Sisters of Mercy Women's Shelter in Mexican Hat?"

She called to Ava Wright, another forensics specialist, who appeared from a neighboring cube. "What's up, Callie?" She glanced at Dylan. "Hi, Acevedo."

He murmured hello. "Did you get the results on that hair I collected from the women's shelter?"

Ava nodded. "It belongs to a Native American male. That's about all I can tell you right now. Bring me a suspect and I can match it."

A Native American? "What about Sherman Watts?"

She shook her head. "Sorry, not a match."

He frowned, his mind spinning. "Did you get anything on the piece of fabric?"

"A denim shirt, cotton blend, inexpensive. The brand is one you'd find at the trading post or a dozen different stores, including online." She drummed her fingers on the table. "So far nothing distinctive about any of it, but I'll keep checking."

"How about the paint samples from my car?"

"We're still working on those."

He pulled the envelope from inside his jacket. "Callie, I stopped by my apartment and found this waiting. Julie must have mailed it to me before she died."

A wary expression made her lips thin. "What's inside?"

He hesitated, not wanting to upset her. After all, the man with her mother in the photo was a big-time criminal. But they had to know what the picture meant and if it was significant.

First though, he showed her the medal, and Callie examined it with gloved hands. "Why did she send Raphael the Archangel to you?" Callie asked.

"He's the patron saint against nightmares." Dylan scrubbed a hand over the back of his neck. "And during the Turnbull case, God knows I had my share of nightmares."

"We all had bad dreams about that one." Callie offered him a sympathetic look, then gestured to the medal. "I'll dust it for prints."

Dylan nodded. "There's something else."

Callie's brow pinched. "What?"

"Look inside."

She hesitated warily, but removed the photograph, her mouth twisting as she studied it. "It's my mother and Vincent Del Gardo."

He nodded, watching as the wheels spun in her head.

Finally a low sound of discomfort escaped her. "Oh, my God." Her gaze rose to meet his, shock settling in the depths of her eyes. "It looks like they knew each other. Like…"

Her sentence trailed off, and Dylan understood the dark place her train of thought had carried her. Del Gardo had his arm around her mother in the photo, and they were both smiling.

As if they had a personal relationship.

Before they could speculate further, Bree and Patrick Martinez entered the room. Patrick was the sheriff of Kenner City and Sabrina a Ute police detective. They'd struck up a romance while investigating Julie's murder and Aspen's disappearance.

"We heard you found Aspen," Bree said. "I'm glad she's alive."

Dylan explained about her amnesia and Bree sighed. "I'll try to stop by and see her. That poor girl and her baby have been through so much."

Patrick grinned and placed his arms around Sabrina's

waist, pulling her up against him. "Speaking of babies. We're going to have one of our own."

"That's wonderful," Callie said. "How far along are you?"

Bree placed a hand over her belly. "Three months."

Dylan congratulated them, although a seed of envy stirred within him.

He hadn't thought much about being a father before, but now that he suspected Jack might be his son, he couldn't think of anything else.

His last encounter with Frank Turnbull flashed back, though, and he grimaced, doubt seeping into places in his mind he didn't like to visit.

Like—maybe he didn't deserve to be a father.

Maybe that was the reason Aspen hadn't contacted him....

She'd met him, *been* with him right after he'd arrested Turnbull. He'd been pent up, so full of rage that he'd admitted that he'd almost killed the man in cold blood.

That he had wanted to inflict pain on Turnbull, make the man suffer before he died.

Hell, he'd tried to pour all that anger and emotion into making love to her, into passion, but there were moments he feared it had bled through.

That he'd frightened her.

"Well, we have rounds to make," Patrick said with a sheepish grin. "Keep us posted on any new evidence. If Perkins and Watts are hiding out on Ute land or in Kenner City, we'll find them. It's only a matter of time."

"Yeah, let's just make that arrest before someone else dies," Dylan growled.

Murmurs of agreement rippled through the room, then they said goodbye.

When Callie turned back, Dylan saw the turmoil on her face as she glanced back at the picture.

But his mind was already straying to the unanswered questions regarding Aspen. He could continue living in a fantasy world, imagining that Jack was his son, or he could find out the truth. And the truth might lead to the unsub after Aspen.

Her safety was all that mattered.

"How about the DNA sample from Jack Meadows?"

Callie and Ava exchanged curious looks. "You think the baby's father might have attacked Aspen?"

He shrugged. "Just covering all the bases. If Watts or Perkins weren't at the shelter, then someone else is after Aspen, too."

"We haven't finished running the DNA," Callie said. "You know paternity tests take time, Dylan."

Frustration knotted his neck. "What if you had a sample to compare it to? Could you at least tell if it was a match?"

"That would help," Ava said. "Do you have one?"

Dylan hesitated, not sure if he wanted to divulge his personal reasons for wanting the test rushed. But he wanted answers. He *needed* answers. And who knew how long it would take for Aspen to remember.

He cleared his throat. "Yeah, mine."

ASPEN FELT ANTSY, as if she was crawling out of her skin. For some reason, having Dylan around had given her a safety net, and although she was comfortable with Emma, the tension of struggling to recall details of her past was draining her. She kept imagining a faceless man attacking her, chasing her, trying to kill her.

Kept wondering who that face belonged to.

Miguel had moved to the porch with his computer and made himself scarce, obviously to give her and Emma privacy. She wondered about her cousin's relationship to Miguel and wanted to ask. Frustration filled her. This was yet another lost part of the past that everyone knew but her.

"You really don't remember anything that happened or how you wound up in that shelter?" Emma asked as they put together a light supper of pasta and salad.

Aspen shook her head, feeling inept, as if she was failing her son. "Not really. But when that car ran us off the road last night, I experienced déjà vu. And I've had nightmares for weeks...."

"I'm so sorry about all this," Emma said quietly. "It must be terribly frustrating."

"It is," Aspen admitted, wringing her hands together. "I don't even remember giving birth. How could a woman possibly forget one of the most important days of her life?"

Emma smiled with compassion. "Maybe you didn't want to remember the labor pain."

Aspen laughed softly. "Were you with me when I was in labor?"

Emma nodded. "Yes. The midwife on the reservation delivered Jack."

Aspen returned to the counter and tossed the salad. "Tell me the truth, Emma. What do you think happened? Why would someone want to hurt me?"

Emma hesitated, her words and tone measured. "How much did Dylan tell you?"

Aspen frowned. "Not much. Just that they thought I might have witnessed a crime."

"That's true," Emma said cautiously.

Aspen seemed to sense she knew much more. "Tell me," Aspen said, almost pleading. "I hate being in the dark like this. Everyone looks at me like I'm a freak."

"You're not a freak," Emma said gently. "But the doctor warned that we should let you remember on your own, not to push you."

Irritation gnawed at Aspen. "It's driving me crazy not knowing." She touched Emma's arm. "Please. I'm not as fragile as everyone thinks. I need to know the truth."

Emma studied her for a moment, then seemed to accept what she'd said and gestured to the kitchen table. "Then sit down, and I'll tell you what I know."

"Thank you." Aspen claimed a kitchen chair while Emma took the one opposite her.

Emma folded her hands on the table. "Dylan and Miguel are brothers. Twins actually. Dylan works for the FBI. Miguel is a forensic specialist for the Kenner County Crime Unit." She hesitated and inhaled a deep breath as if to fortify herself, and Aspen realized that her disappearance had deeply upset her cousin. But before she voiced her concerns and an apology, Emma continued.

"One of their friends, a federal agent named Julie Grainger, was murdered during the process of an ongoing investigation into Vincent Del Gardo, a major crime boss. The FBI believe that a hit man named Boyd Perkins killed Del Gardo and Julie." She paused as if weighing her words and Aspen encouraged her to continue.

"They found evidence that you might have witnessed a hit man, Boyd Perkins, who worked with a man named

Sherman Watts, a local Ute man, dumping Julie's body. Apparently they saw you and chased you, causing you to crash. We thought you'd drowned in the river, but somehow you must have escaped."

Aspen massaged her temple, the horrific images of fighting the river current sending a shudder through her. "That makes sense. I've had dreams about nearly drowning and being chased."

Emma closed her hand over Aspen's. "I'm so sorry, honey."

Aspen squeezed Emma's fingers. "So how did you and Miguel get involved?"

A faraway look settled in Emma's eyes, one that indicated that Emma did see things more deeply than others. "When they found your car, Jack was inside. They brought him to me to keep until we found out what happened to you." Emma traced a finger along the hand woven placement. "Because of my visions, they had me visit the place where your car crashed. I sensed that you were alive, but I couldn't see anything specific to help."

Aspen's chest clenched at the frustration in her cousin's words. "I'm sorry. That must have been difficult for you, Emma."

Aspen swallowed. Moisture gathered in Emma's eyes. "Yes, it was. I was so afraid you were dead...."

"No, I'm all right. And thank you for taking care of Jack for me."

"I love him, Aspen. You two are the only family I have."

Aspen hugged her, the two of them bonding, memories of other times when she and Emma had shared problems surfacing. Aspen traced a finger over Emma's hair, pushing it back behind her ear. "So tell me about you and Miguel."

Emma dabbed at her eyes, then glanced toward the porch. "Miguel was working the case with Dylan. At first he didn't believe me, but then I led him to the gutter where we found a Native American leather necklace in the snow. That's how they connected Perkins to Watts and to you."

Aspen's mind raced. "So I was just in the wrong place at the wrong time?"

"I'm afraid so," Emma said. "Then…"

"Then what?"

Fear darkened Emma's eyes. "One night I had a vision and went back to the river, hoping to remember more. But Sherman Watts was there and tried to kill me."

Aspen clasped her hand. "Oh, my God."

Emma shivered. "I was terrified, but Miguel showed up and saved me."

"And he's been hanging around ever since," Aspen said with a smile.

Emma blushed and ducked her head. "Yes, we've grown close."

"I'm glad you found someone," Aspen said sincerely. "He certainly seems protective of you."

Emma blushed again. "Yes, well… Apparently the Feds think that Watts and Perkins are hiding out on the reservation somewhere. They're afraid he'll come back for me and for you." She glanced up at Aspen with terror streaking her face. "Apparently they did come after you."

The breath in Aspen's lungs tightened.

"But don't worry," Emma said. "Miguel will protect me, and I know that Dylan will stay with you until the men are arrested."

Aspen shifted, threading her fingers together. The thought of Dylan protecting her made her uneasy. He seemed angry, intense…and darkly sexy.

She was attracted to him in a way that she sensed she hadn't been attracted to another man before.

The sound of an engine jerked her from her thoughts, and Emma went to the door while Aspen glanced out the window. Speaking of the devil, the sexy agent was back. She could practically see the chords of muscle playing on his chest beneath that gun holster. Could feel the power radiating off of him.

Dylan met Miguel on the steps, both speaking in hushed tones that made her wonder what he'd learned at the crime lab.

A second later, a big black truck parked in the drive and a tall Indian climbed out, his sun-streaked ponytail accentuating a lean angular face. He was tanned and lanky, his body coiled with tension. "Who's that?" Aspen asked.

"Kurt Lightfoot," Emma said. "He works for the Weeminuche Construction Authority. He's very adamant about enforcing the code that all projects are performed on a merit shop basis with maximum use of Native American laborers and craftsmen."

"Do I know him?" Aspen asked.

Emma's face twisted. "Yes. You've gone out a few times."

Aspen's head throbbed with all the revelations. How well did she know Kurt? And how did she feel about him?

Dylan's stance turned protective, and he blocked the doorway, his arms crossed, his muscular legs spread wide. She imagined him interrogating Kurt and felt a margin of relief that he was present, that she didn't have to face this other man alone.

The tunnel of darkness into which she'd fallen seemed endless and growing deeper and more frightening every second. If she'd dated Kurt, why would she be afraid of him?

A tense heartbeat passed, then the three men stepped inside, Miguel and Dylan on each side of Kurt, like armed guards—or cobras ready to strike. "There's someone here to see you," Dylan said, although distrust and something even darker laced his voice.

Anger?

A smile broadened Kurt's angular face and he strode over and pulled her into his arms, then spoke in the ancient language of their ancestors. "Thank the gods, I'm glad you're home."

She studied him, trying to place him in her lost past. "What are you doing here?"

He cupped her face in his hands and kissed her briefly.

She forced herself not to react, waiting for some kind of response to shift inside her, for a pleasant memory to surface, for her to want this man.

But no sparks flew, no tingle of attraction or passion stirred as it had when Dylan Acevedo had first looked into her eyes at that shelter.

He pulled away slightly, examining her with narrowed eyes. "I came to see you and Jack," he said. "I've missed you both so much."

Distrust flooded her along with another disturbing thought. Could Kurt possibly be Jack's father?

And if so, why did she feel no attraction to him, only the need to put distance between them?

DYLAN BARELY BIT BACK A CURSE.

This big Indian in the suede-fringed jacket was the man Aspen had been dating? And he had just kissed her as if he owned her.

Pure rage ripped through him like an out-of-control brush fire, eating him alive. He fisted his hands and started to yank the man away from her, but Miguel caught his arm and gave him a warning look that reminded him of when they were teenagers after Teresa had died, and Dylan had been quick-tempered, spoiling for a fight.

Dammit. His brother was right. He was acting like a crazed, jealous husband, when he had no claims on Aspen.

But what if he wanted to have claims on her?

And what if Jack was his?

To fill the awkward silence, Emma rallied to explain about Lightfoot's work for the WCA, making his anger mount. Dammit, the guy sounded like a stand-up man.

But not everyone was as honorable as they appeared on the surface. Plus, the hair he'd collected at the shelter when Aspen had been attacked belonged to a Native American. What if Lightfoot had tracked down Aspen and broken into her room?

He'd have to get a warrant to compare his DNA.

And until he found the answers he needed, he'd stick by Aspen 24/7.

Aspen took a step back, and massaged her temple as if fighting a headache. "Jack fell asleep. I don't want to disturb him."

Lightfoot shoved his hands in the pockets of his faded jeans. "Of course. How are you feeling?"

"Actually I'm tired." Aspen's gaze flitted to Emma, then to him as if pleading for a way out.

"We had an accident on the way back last night," Dylan said, jumping in to circumvent a long stay by the other man. "The doctor gave her a clean bill of health, but she didn't get much rest."

Aspen nodded and rubbed at her head again. "Maybe we could visit another time, Kurt. I need to lie down for a while."

"I don't mind staying," Lightfoot offered with a shrug. "I can sleep on the couch and be here if Jack wakes up."

"That won't be necessary," Dylan cut in. "I'm Aspen's bodyguard until the threat to her is over and the men who attacked her are in jail."

Anger glinted in Lightfoot's eyes a second before he masked it. "Good. Nice to know the FBI is doing their job instead of ignoring us Utes."

Anger shot through Dylan at Lightfoot's implication, but again, Miguel held him in check with a forceful look.

Aspen excused herself and went to her room, and Lightfoot shifted uncomfortably, glancing at the nursery as if he wanted to go in. As if he had a right.

But Emma took him by the arm and diplomatically led him to the door. "Why don't you come back once she's had time to rest and adjust."

Dylan waited until she walked him outside, then went to Aspen's door, knocked and pushed it open a fraction. "He's gone. Are you all right?"

"Yes." Jack stirred and Aspen rushed to the nursery then returned, cradling him as if she'd never let him go again while Emma finished preparing dinner and set it on the table.

The meal was strained, and Aspen appeared fatigued, so Emma and Miguel said good-night afterward. Dylan insisted on cleaning up while Aspen fed Jack, then he watched as she read him a story, sang a Ute lullaby to him and rocked him to sleep.

His chest grew hollow with the fear that this family wasn't his to have, an ache so deep inside him that he didn't know what he'd do if he had to walk away from her and her son.

Yet what if she didn't want him in her life when the investigation ended? What if there was another man, either Lightfoot or someone else, who had stolen her heart while he'd stayed away?

Jack fell asleep and she tucked the baby into the crib, then yawned, and Dylan encouraged her to go to bed.

But, dammit, he wanted to join her. If he touched her, held her, kissed her, would she remember what they'd shared?

Of course, he did none of that. He was working a case, and staying alert meant keeping his emotional distance.

And protecting his heart.

But after forty-eight hours with no sleep, exhaustion finally claimed him, and he stretched out on her sofa and fell asleep, dreaming about the night he and Aspen had met.

But sometime around 4:00 a.m., he jerked awake, his senses on full alert, his heart pounding.

Had he heard something outside?

A scream?

Aspen or Jack crying out?

He grabbed his gun off the coffee table, rose and checked Aspen's room, but she seemed to be resting. He tiptoed to the nursery, but when he peeked inside, Jack was sound asleep.

Nerves cramping his chest, he went back to the den, eased back the window curtain and looked outside. Darkness bathed the property, the stillness almost alarming in its own right. In the distance a motor rumbled, and a prairie dog wailed its call.

Dylan had to check outside.

Senses honed, he inched to the front door, unlocked it and slowly cracked the door open, the chain still intact. His gaze shot sideways, searching, scanning, his fingers gripping his weapon, ready to fire.

A stray cat trotted across the dirt, and dust swirled in a cloud from the road in the distance as if a car had just roared away. He glanced down at the porch and an icy chill rippled through his blood.

Frank Turnbull's calling card—a piece of thunderwood lay at his feet.

No…it couldn't be possible. Turnbull was supposed to be in jail….

Chapter Seven

She was drowning.

The raging, icy current dragged her under, slamming her already battered body against the rocks. Pain shot through her limbs and head, and she battled for a breath but the water slapped her face and she choked.

She opened her eyes, saw the bottom of the river, felt the murky floor sucking at her feet, mud seeping into her shoes, the darkness swirling above her. Her head throbbed, her lungs aching as if they were going to explode....

What had happened?

A faint memory stirred. The car crash. Then the men chasing her...clubbing her in the head...then the black emptiness.

And now the icy river, her burial spot.

Her lungs squeezed, desperate for oxygen, and she was fading, her energy waning. She wasn't going to make it.

Terror crawled through her.

No...she didn't want to die.

She was a good swimmer—she had to make her arms

and legs work. Push away the numbness, forget the pain. One stroke, then another.

She had to survive. Someone was waiting on her. Someone important.

Determination raged through her, and she fought the waves, using her feet for momentum to push off the bottom and propel herself upward. Suddenly she was moving, swimming again. Her lungs begged for air, and her teeth chattered, but she ignored the burning ache and pushed harder.

One stroke, two, three, kick, kick, kick… She imagined the night sky above, the stars, a sliver of moonlight… Warmth.

So beautiful. She would see it again. She would feel warm and safe. Then she'd go home. Home to…home to something…

Finally she broke the surface, gasping for air. Light and cold air swirled around her, disorienting her as to which way to swim. She struggled to orient herself. The current tugged at her again, and she let it carry her forward.

Finally, through the shadows she spotted trees in the distance and kicked harder, aiming for the shore. Another stroke. Another. She could do it. She would make it to the edge and climb out.

Someone was waiting on her. Someone important. Someone who loved her and needed her to survive.

And then she was there, the riverbank only inches away. She reached for the edge, lost her footing and slipped under again. But sheer determination spiked her adrenaline and she kicked to the surface. Her arms shook as she clawed at a tree branch and used it to drag herself to the bank. Coughing and spitting out water, she collapsed in a fit of exhaustion, shivering and shaking, too numb to move.

A second later, fear shot through her again.

But this time she was in the bed, and a man was lurching toward her. A knife glinted in the darkness.

She screamed, and kicked at him as he approached. She'd survived once, she could do it again.

His angular face filled the darkness, his breath hissing across her cheek as he grabbed her. A sliver of moonlight caught his profile. He had high cheekbones. Long hair.

He was an Indian.

But who was he? And why did he want her dead?

DYLAN HAD JUST BAGGED the piece of thunderwood when Aspen's scream shattered the silence. He slammed the front door shut, grabbed his gun and raced to her bedroom, sweat beading on his neck.

What if Turnbull had escaped? What if he'd gotten in to Aspen's room?

Darkness bathed the room, so he flipped on the light, quickly searching for the intruder. But he didn't see one.

A quick glance at the window confirmed it was closed.

Aspen was sitting up in bed, trembling as she rocked herself back and forth.

He inhaled a steadying breath, stowed his gun in the waistband of his slacks, then walked over to the bed. "Aspen…"

She jerked her head toward him, her terror-glazed eyes wrenching his heart.

"What happened?" he asked gruffly. "Are you all right?"

For a moment, she simply stared at him as if she hadn't

understood what he'd said. Hating to see her in agony, he inched closer to the bed, wanting to console her.

"You're safe now," he said as he slowly lowered himself to the mattress beside her. "I won't let anyone hurt you again." He stroked her arms gently, aching to hold her. "Was someone here in the room?"

Her face seemed to crumple but she shook her head no, her teeth chattering. "I was running from a man, then he hit me over the head and threw me in the river. Then I was drowning," she whispered. "Drowning in the icy water. It was so cold...and I couldn't breathe."

"It was a dream, a memory of your attack," he said. "But you're safe in your house now."

She shoved a tangled strand of hair from her damp cheek. "I fought, had to swim, to escape. And then I was in the room at the shelter and that man was there. He had a knife and he came after me."

In light of the piece of thunderwood on her doorstep, her reference to a knife sent alarm down his spine. "Could you describe the knife?"

She frowned, her eyes narrowing as if in thought.

"Could it have been a Ute ceremonial knife? Was it made of white quartz and cedar wood?"

"I don't know. I didn't get a look at it," she said in a hoarse voice.

He tilted up her chin, forcing her to look at him. "What else do you remember, Aspen?"

"He was an Indian," she said. "I think I might have seen him before. Maybe hanging around the shelter."

Hope sprouted inside him. If she'd seen him, at least he'd know who to go after. "Was it the same man who threw you in the river?"

She clenched the sheet between her fingers. "No… I'm not sure."

Maybe he should show her some photos, see if they jogged her memory. But the doctor had warned him not to push. "Do you remember any more details, the color of his hair, his height?"

Her eyes were glazed as she stared up at him. "He had long hair, high cheekbones—I think he might have been Kurt Lightfoot."

He clenched his jaw. Maybe his theory about Lightfoot being Jack's father was on target. Maybe he hadn't wanted to claim the child and he'd tracked down Aspen at the shelter to silence her.

Then he'd shown up at Aspen's to test her to see if her amnesia was real.

Which meant he had to be nervous.

Dylan gave her arm a reassuring squeeze. "All right. I'll get a warrant for a DNA sample from him and run a background check. We can compare the DNA to the hair I found at the shelter."

He started to get up, but she grabbed his hand, clinging to him, and heat bolted through him. She was vulnerable now, not asking for a repeat of their Vegas week.

Although he couldn't erase the erotic images from his mind.

But if Jack is yours, she didn't tell you.

His anger returned, sharp and intense, and he steeled himself against feeling anything else. He had a job to do and he'd damn well do it.

"But what if I'm wrong?" Aspen said. "I don't want to accuse an innocent man of something he didn't do."

He frowned, wondering if she might have had feelings for the man. "Trust me to see just how innocent Lightfoot is."

Her big dark eyes studied him, probing, looking lost.

She finally nodded, and his breath whooshed out in relief. "I'm going to call and get a security system installed today. I want you and Jack to stay at Emma's while I go back to the crime lab."

"All right."

He stepped outside and phoned the warden at the Colorado State Penitentiary. Sweat beaded on his neck as he waited to be patched through to his office.

It seemed like an eternity before the man answered in a thick Hispanic accent. "Warden Fernandez."

"Warden, this is Special Agent Dylan Acevedo."

A long sigh echoed over the line. "You were on my list to call today."

That didn't sound good. "Really. About Frank Turnbull? Has he escaped?"

Another tense pause. "We're not certain. We think he may be dead."

Dead? God, he hoped to hell the man was.

"What do you mean, you *think* he may be?"

"Yesterday he was on a bus with three other prisoners we were transferring to the ADX in Florence."

The ADX, the Alcatraz of the Rockies, where the prisoners deemed most dangerous and in need of tightest control were locked away. The home of the notorious Terry Nichols, Eric Robert Rudolph, Timothy McVeigh and Richard Reid, the shoe bomber.

The air in Dylan's lungs stilled. "And?"

"And the bus had an accident, caught on fire and exploded. There were six people on board—the driver, two guards and three prisoners. We found six bodies. So we're assuming Turnbull died in the accident, but the ME is studying the remains. That's going to take time, though. Wasn't much left but charred skin and bones. He's requested dental and medical records to verify the IDs."

"Tell him to rush it," Dylan said.

"You don't have to remind me. These were all lifers who needed maximum security."

Dylan pulled a hand down his chin. Two others as mean as Turnbull. Not good.

"We're investigating the accident to make sure it wasn't an attempted prison escape or sabotage from an outsider."

Damn, that would create panic.

"How did you find out?" Fernandez asked. "We've tried to keep it quiet so as not to frighten locals."

People needed to be warned. "I'm on the Ute Reservation, investigating the murder of one of our agents and working protective custody of a Ute woman. Early this morning, I found a piece of thunderwood on her doorstep."

"Turnbull's calling card," Fernandez muttered.

"Exactly." And Aspen fit the profile. Plus, Turnbull had vowed to get revenge on Dylan at his trial.

"Could be a copycat. Someone who knows you worked the case trying to yank your chain."

"I know. But we need to verify that Turnbull didn't escape," Dylan said, trying to focus. "If he has, he's been planning it and may have had help from the outside. I want to look at all his prison correspondence. Because if he's out, he'll start his crime spree all over again."

And he had to stop him before any more women died.

ASPEN MANAGED TO GRAB A SHOWER, dress and make coffee before Jack woke up, although her muscles and limbs were still sore. The sound of her son cooing brought a smile to her lips, and she hurried to the nursery and stood over him, soaking in his features.

This was her child. Her little boy with the thick jet-black hair, brown skin and high cheekbones. He definitely had her Ute blood.

Except for those startling deep blue eyes…

He waved his hands and kicked his feet, and she picked him up and hugged him to her chest, savoring the sweet scent of baby powder and softness. "Good morning, little one. You're in a good mood today."

"Maybe because he's happy to have his mother home," Dylan said behind her.

Her chest squeezed. "Poor little guy must have thought I'd abandoned him."

"He seems resilient," Dylan said.

She carried Jack to the changing table and unsnapped the legs of his sleeper, laughing as he tried to put his toes in his mouth. "You silly boy, you. You can't eat your feet."

Dylan walked over and watched him for a moment, an odd look on his face. But a knock sounded at the door and he quickly left to answer it.

She finished the diaper change and snapped his jimmies, then carried him to the kitchen and retrieved a bottle while Dylan let two men from the security company he'd called inside to install the security system.

While they worked on the installation, she placed Jack in his baby seat, then made breakfast, pancakes with the fresh blueberries Emma had stored in the refrigerator.

Jack cooed and shook a toy rattle between his pudgy

fingers while they ate, intrigued by Dylan when he turned to talk to him. But tension stretched between them, a silence filled with the questions she couldn't answer.

"Thank you for breakfast," Dylan said as he finished the stack of hotcakes and carried his plate to the sink. He rinsed it and placed it in the dishwasher, then started to clean up the pan.

"I'll take care of that," Aspen said, a warmth enveloping her. It felt oddly comforting to share breakfast with the man. Comforting and sexy…

And vaguely familiar, as if they'd done it before.

"Then I'm going to give Jack a bath before we go to Emma's."

Dylan nodded. "I phoned Miguel and told him you were coming."

"Thanks."

The workers finished with the security system, and Dylan explained how to set the alarm and deactivate it. "You need to leave it on at all times, even when you're home."

She nodded, picked up Jack and took him to her bathroom to bathe him. But anxiety plucked at her nerves. She didn't want to live in fear for the rest of her life.

She just hoped that Dylan found the person after her soon so life could return to normal. Maybe then her memories would surface, and she'd remember who Jack's father was and why he wasn't in her son's life.

AFTER THE SECURITY TEAM LEFT, Dylan drove Aspen and Jack to Emma's. Unlike, Aspen's house with its

Native American look and feel, Emma's was a small ranch, the furnishings eclectic and more modern.

Aspen carried Jack inside and Dylan followed. Emma had set up a crib in the second bedroom along with baby paraphernalia, and eagerly welcomed her cousin and son inside. From the loving expression on Emma's face, she'd grown quite attached to Jack during their time together.

Aspen smiled gratefully as they settled in to visit, although her features were still strained.

Dylan gestured to the door. "Miguel, can I talk to you outside for a minute?"

Miguel nodded, his eyes narrowing as they moved to the front porch. "What's up?"

Dylan explained about the piece of thunderwood and his conversation with the warden.

"Good God," Miguel muttered. "You think Turnbull may have escaped?"

Dylan shrugged. "I don't know, but we have to consider the possibility."

Miguel grunted. "Jeez. This just keeps getting worse. Now we're not only hunting Perkins and Watts but possibly an escaped felon."

Dylan grimaced. "Yeah, and not just a felon, a man who likes to carve up Ute women."

Miguel's face paled. "I was on my way into the crime lab today for work. But I hate to leave Emma and Aspen alone."

"We can't," Dylan said. "If you need to go in, call the locals to dispatch a unit out here until I get back."

"Where are you going?" Miguel asked.

"Last night Aspen remembered that the man who attacked her at the shelter was Indian. The crime lab has a hair I found at the shelter. I want to get a warrant for a DNA sample from Kurt Lightfoot to see if it belongs to him."

"Did they compare it to Watts's?"

Dylan nodded. "No match. And the hair could have been there before. Or the man who came in could be one of the abusers another woman at the shelter was running from. But if it's Lightfoot's, then I can bring him in for questioning."

"I'll call Bree," Miguel said. "Ask her to watch Emma and Aspen. It sounds like the lab needs me now."

Dylan nodded. "Thanks, man. And if you don't mind, check with the state ME and see if he's ID'ed the bodies from the prison bus. We need to know if one of them is Turnbull's."

HE STUDIED THE PHOTO of Aspen Meadows, his hands twitching to finish her off. She should have died in that river, but she was stronger than anyone thought. Had fought her way out of the raging current and wound up being rescued.

Those stark features, her high cheekbones, long black hair, big brown eyes—the Ute woman had seen too much with those eyes.

The paper said she had amnesia. But her memory could return at any minute.

Then she'd squeal on him and he'd rot in prison.

No, he wouldn't get caught.

Rage shot through his blood, and he tensed and drew

an X over the picture. Frustrated, he crumpled the paper in his hands and threw it against the wall.

Yes, Aspen Meadows had to die. The sooner the better.

And he'd make sure the end was painful….

Chapter Eight

On the way to the Kenner County Crime Lab, Dylan phoned Tom Ryan and asked him to assemble the other agents and crime scene specialists for a meeting in the conference room.

Ben Parrish and Tom Ryan were the first to join him and Miguel, then Callie, Ava, Jerry Griswold and Bart Flemming appeared.

"Griffin Vaughn, his son, Luke, and new wife, Sophie, have come to Kenner City," Ben said.

"Interesting," Tom commented.

Everyone looked exhausted and frustrated as if they'd worked too many hours for too many weeks now with no hope of seeing the end in sight.

But he and Tom and Ben had been friends with Julie and had vowed to avenge her death.

And Aspen's safety was personal. *Very* personal.

Tom grabbed a cup of coffee and rapped his knuckles on the table to get everyone's attention. "Let's have an update. Any leads on where Sherman Watts and Boyd Perkins are hiding out?"

Ben shook his head. "No spottings. They could be

anywhere." He paused with a hand gesture. "Or long gone by now."

Dylan grimaced. "I doubt that. With Aspen alive, they'll want to tie up loose ends. The fingerprint we found at the Griffin estate points to the fact that Perkins shot Del Gardo and that he's a hired gun with the Wayne crime family." Dylan gestured toward Jerry. "Griswold identified the bullet casings from my vehicle as coming from a .38. Could have been from Watts's gun." He glanced at Ava. "How about the paint samples from the car that ran me off the road?"

Ava consulted her notes. "They match the samples we found on Aspen's car, the ones that belong to Watts's vehicle."

Dammit. "So they are after her," he said, and everyone exchanged frustrated looks. So far Watts and Perkins had been as invisible as Ute ghosts.

"There's another complication," he continued, then gestured to the whiteboard where they were keeping lists of all the clues, evidence and suspects. "The hair I found in the room at the Sisters of Mercy Women's Shelter where Aspen was attacked belonged to an Indian, but not Watts. So we're also looking for another suspect."

"Why would someone else want to harm Aspen?" Ben asked.

Dylan added Kurt Lightfoot's name to the board. "We're not sure yet. But a Ute man named Kurt Lightfoot has shown interest in Aspen and her son." He hesitated then continued, forcing his emotions at bay as he glanced at Callie. "Do we have an ID on the baby's father?"

Callie shook her head. "Hopefully soon."

Dylan tugged at his shirt collar. "Apparently Lightfoot and Aspen dated for a while. I'm not sure how, or if the relationship ended but we need to check him out." He directed his attention to Bart, their computer analyst. "Lightfoot works for the Weeminuche Construction Authority. Dig up everything you can find on him."

"Will do," Bart said with a nod.

"And, Ryan," Dylan said. "I need a warrant for Lightfoot's DNA."

"You'll have it before you leave today," Tom said. "And, Bart, make that background check on the man a priority. I may need it for the warrant."

Bart stood. "I'll get on it now."

"Wait," Dylan said before he could exit the room. "There's something else."

Concerned looks floated around the room, then Dylan explained. "Frank Turnbull, the Ute Slicer, was being transported from the Colorado State Pen to the ADX Florence when his bus crashed and burned. Six charred bodies were found in the van. It appears Turnbull may have died, but the ME's analyzing the remains now to confirm. Until we have confirmation, we have to work under the assumption that he might have escaped."

"And you're basing that on what?" Ava asked.

Sweat trickled down the back of Dylan's neck. "On the piece of thunderwood someone left on Aspen Meadow's doorstep."

Startled gasps and low curses met his announcement. "Jesus, people will panic if this news leaks out," Ava said.

"Maybe we should issue a warning so the Ute women will be careful," Callie suggested.

Tom gave a brisk shake of his head. "Not until we know more."

"I'm going to push the ME," Miguel said. "See if we can get answers on that ID ASAP."

Callie gestured to speak. "I'll drive up there and offer my help. Won't hurt to have a set of our eyes on the investigation there."

"Thanks, Callie." Dylan felt marginally better knowing she'd be breathing down their necks. "I requested all of Turnbull's prison correspondence for analysis. I'm going to look at his visitors, letters, phone calls, e-mails, along with any inmates who might have befriended him," Dylan said. "If this so-called accident was the result of an attempted prison break, we need to find out."

"You think someone on the outside might have helped him escape?" Ben asked.

"It's possible. Let's face it. Turnbull didn't get away with ten murders before we stopped him because he's dumb. He's cunning, manipulative, well organized, a methodical cold-blooded killer. We all know the kind of violence he's capable of." He paused, wiping at his brow as he tried to banish the images of the dead girls from his mind. "And we all also know that some women get off on writing prisoners. If he has a fan club, I want to know about it."

"Good point," Tom said.

"And if Turnbull is dead?" Ben asked.

Dylan was sweating again. "Then we may have a copycat on our hands." He hesitated. "And Aspen fits the profile. With all the hype about her disappearance, and me working the case, he might come after her."

"All the more reason to smoke out anyone else who's after her," Ben mumbled.

Tom met his gaze, his brow pinching. "I agree. Dylan, I've been thinking about what you said. That Perkins and Watts won't stop until they kill Aspen."

A cold knot of anxiety clawed at Dylan's insides as tension thrummed through the room. "And?"

Tom's gaze turned to stone, and Dylan knew he wasn't going to like whatever Tom suggested.

"This mess has gone on way too long. We're all tired of chasing our asses and coming up with nothing." He planted his hands on the conference table and gave Dylan a dead-serious look. "I think we should consider setting a trap for the men. Flesh them out."

Dylan gritted his teeth. "How do you suggest we do that?"

Tom shrugged as if the answer was inevitable. "We use Aspen as bait."

ASPEN FED JACK HIS BOTTLE while Emma prepared lunch, a well of sadness engulfing her as she thought of the weeks she'd lost with her little boy. "The word *Ute* comes from the Spanish name for our tribe, Yuta," she said softly as Jack gazed up at her. "Most Utes speak English, but I'll try to teach you a few of the words of our Native language."

Jack splayed one little hand on the edge of the bottle and sucked vigorously. Apparently her son had a good appetite and seemed to be healthy despite the situation.

"The word *maiku* is a friendly greeting, and *tog'oiak'* means thank you." She stroked his thick black hair. "A long time ago our people lived in wickiups. They were small round houses shaped like a cone and made of a willow frame covered with brush. But times have changed and now we live in houses on a reservation." She laughed as he squirmed against her, grateful she hadn't forgotten her heritage. "A long time ago we traveled the rivers by building rafts. And we still like to hunt and fish. When you get big enough, I'll take you to see the Bear Dance and the Sun Dance at Mesa Verde, and as you grow up, I'll teach you more about the Ute ceremonies and how to use roots and plants for healing."

Bree smiled at her from the kitchen where she was slicing fruit for a fruit salad. But the gun at the detective's waist reminded her of the real reason Bree had stopped by.

"You're a wonderful mother, Aspen," Bree said.

Suddenly an image of her and Emma drifted into Aspen's consciousness. The two of them as little girls playing with their dolls on the reservation. Then another, she and Emma skipping after her mother to the trading post. Her mother buying penny candy for them as a treat. Emma being quiet, shy, almost withdrawn at times. Emma finally confiding that sometimes she saw things she didn't want to see.

Like her mother's boyfriend hitting her.

And then her grandmother's ghost…

She glanced up as Emma placed salads and herbal tea on the table. "Emma?"

Her face must have revealed her concern because Emma rushed to the table and sat down. "What is it?"

"A memory…I think."

"Of the man who attacked you?" Emma asked, and Bree paused at the kitchen counter to study her.

Aspen shook her head. "No. Of you and me when we were young. What happened to your mother?"

Emma's face paled, and she knotted her hands on the table.

Jack was dozing so she eased him into the baby seat, then reached out and squeezed Emma's hand. "I'm sorry. I didn't mean to bring up a painful subject."

Emma sighed. "No, it's all right. It was a long time ago." She took a deep breath. "My mother's boyfriend abused her. One night they got in a terrible fight, and he set the house on fire. Both of them died."

"That's right. I had a memory about a fire," Aspen said.

"That's when I came to live with you and Aunt Rose."

Rose…her mother's name. An image of her face flashed back, bittersweet and painful because it felt as it was so long ago. As if it was another thing lost. Maybe forever.

"And my mother? She's dead?"

Emma's gaze met hers, tears glittering in her eyes. "Yes, Rose died last year of cancer. Right before you went to Las Vegas to finish school."

"And my father?"

"He was never in the picture. I think that's why you were so determined that you could handle raising Jack alone."

The rumble of a motor startled them all, and Bree held up a warning hand, indicating for them to wait, then removed her weapon from her holster and went to the window.

"Is it Miguel or Dylan?"

"Neither," Bree said. "Kurt Lightfoot."

Aspen tensed. Emma had said that she and Kurt had dated. And she had wondered if he had been the man she'd seen at the shelter, the one who'd attacked her.

"Should we let him in?" Emma asked.

Bree shrugged. "I've known Kurt for a while. I don't think he's dangerous, if that's what you're worried about."

She opened the door, and Kurt's voice echoed from the porch. "I came to talk to Aspen. I figured if she wasn't at home, she might be with Emma."

"She is," Bree said, then gestured for him to come in.

Kurt shifted awkwardly as his gaze met hers. He was a handsome man, she supposed. Tall and muscular, and from what she'd been told, he was doing good things for the reservation by working for the WCA. But his gaze bore into hers as if she'd betrayed him by forgetting him.

And the dream of the Indian man attacking her haunted her….

"Can we talk in private?" he asked.

Aspen glanced at Emma, then Bree, and Emma gestured to Jack who'd stirred from sleep and was cooing at her. "Bree and I will take Jack out on the porch for a minute. If that's all right with you, Aspen?"

Aspen reluctantly nodded. If Kurt was dangerous, he certainly wouldn't try to hurt her with the detective and Emma present.

She dropped a kiss on her son's forehead, hating to let him go. She'd missed so much already. But Emma gently cradled him in her arms and whispered to him as she carried him outside, and Aspen took comfort in knowing that he was only a few feet away.

She'd never lose him again.

Kurt waited until Bree joined Emma before he claimed the chair beside her. "How are you feeling?"

"I'm doing all right, just frustrated that I can't remember my life." She twined her fingers together, nerves knotting her stomach.

"I'm sorry. I didn't come to push you," Kurt said in a deep voice. "I just wanted you to know that I'm here if you need me." He reached out and squeezed her hand, and a ripple of unease tripped through her.

"I care about you, Aspen. You may not remember it, but we were…are good friends." His lips curled into a smile. "In fact, we've been more than that."

Her gaze shot to his, probing, searching for the truth. "What are you saying?"

"That we talked about a future together, about marriage," he said quietly. "About me moving in and taking care of you and little Jack."

Confusion clouded her head as she struggled to recall that conversation and the relationship Kurt implied they'd had. Had she considered marrying Kurt? Had she been in love with him?

And if she had, why did she feel more drawn to Dylan Acevedo, the federal agent who was protecting her and Jack than Kurt?

"What about Jack's birth father?" Aspen asked. "Did I tell you who he was?" He stroked his thumb over her hand.

"No," Kurt said, glancing down at her fingers, which were curled into a knot. "But that doesn't matter to me, Aspen. I'll love Jack and raise him as my own."

She chewed over his words. "Did I say anything about Jack's father?"

A frown marred Kurt's face, causing wrinkles to crease across his forehead. "You said you didn't tell him about the pregnancy because you were frightened of him," Kurt said. "And that he'd never know about your son."

The front door squeaked open, and Aspen glanced up to see Dylan standing in the door, a thunderous expression slashing his chiseled face.

IT TOOK EVERY OUNCE of Dylan's restraint not to lunge forward and rip Lightfoot's hands off of Aspen. Aspen had told Lightfoot she was afraid of the baby's father. Had she been afraid of him?

Or another man?

He folded his arms. "What are you doing here, Lightfoot?"

The Indian didn't budge, but Aspen slipped her hands down to her lap, twisting them together.

"I came to see Aspen and Jack," Lightfoot said with a scowl.

"About what?"

"I care about her," he said matter-of-factly. "I figured that she needed her friends now."

"She does need her friends," Dylan cut in sharply, "but I'm not sure you're one of them."

Lightfoot took a step closer as if he had no intention of backing down. "What makes you say that?"

Dylan held up the warrant. "The fact that we found a hair belonging to a male Native American in the room where Aspen was attacked at the women's shelter where she was recuperating."

A sarcastic expression curled Lightfoot's mouth. "In case you haven't noticed, I'm not the only male Indian in this part of the country."

Dylan shrugged. "Still, I'll need a DNA sample."

His tone challenged him to decline. "For elimination purposes, of course."

Lightfoot threw up his hands in warning as Dylan stalked toward him. "Wait a minute, you have no right."

Dylan smiled. The hell he didn't. "This warrant says I do."

"How did you obtain a warrant?" Lightfoot asked. "I've done nothing wrong, nothing suspicious."

The fact that he was all over Aspen was enough to make Dylan hate his guts. "The judge saw differently. Now about that sample?"

A muscle ticked in Lightfoot's jaw, then he growled. "You don't need to take a sample."

"Why not?" Dylan asked.

"Because I was there," Lightfoot admitted. "In Mexican Hat."

Chapter Nine

"You broke into the room at the shelter?" Aspen asked.

Kurt reached for her but Aspen backed away from his touch. "It's not what you think."

"It sounds to me like you attacked her," Dylan suggested.

"No," Kurt said harshly. "You've got it all wrong."

"But you grabbed me," Aspen said. "I didn't make that up."

"I didn't attack you," Kurt argued. "I only wanted to talk to you, to make sure you were all right, but you panicked and started screaming. Then everyone ran in and I figured I had to get out of there before a dozen women pounced on me."

Aspen frowned, struggling to make sense of his explanation and debating over what to believe. She'd been terrified, having nightmares, and then she'd seen a man sneaking into her room.

Could she have mistaken his intent?

"We're not buying that story," Dylan said. "If you wanted to talk to her, you would have gone to the door like a normal person. Besides, how did you find her when the police hadn't located her yet?"

"I can explain." Kurt shifted nervously, one hand running over the length of that leather pouch. The one holding the knife Aspen had seen.

Dylan studied the man's body language, his senses on alert in case Lightfoot decided to attack. Kurt pressed his hand over the pouch.

"Don't even think about it," Dylan warned.

Kurt's gaze shot up. "Think about what?"

"About using the knife." Dylan gestured for him to remove the weapon and hand it over. Kurt muttered an obscenity, but gave him the knife.

Then he turned to Aspen. "Let me explain. Please."

Dylan pointed to the kitchen chair. "Sit down. And put your hands on the table in front of you where I can see them."

Kurt did as Dylan instructed, but gave Aspen a desperate look. "Please listen to me. I would never hurt you, Aspen."

Aspen frowned. "Then explain why you broke in my room and scared me to death."

"I'm sorry I frightened you." Kurt glanced at Dylan with wary eyes. "Aspen and I had been seeing each other for the last few months, ever since she moved back from Vegas to the reservation. But she confided that she was afraid of Jack's father, that he wasn't Ute, and that if he discovered he had a son, he might try to take Jack away from her."

The scar on Dylan's chin twitched with a frown. "So you aren't the baby's father?"

Kurt shook his head. "I offered to be, though." He glanced at Aspen with a soulful look. "I wish you remembered. I wanted to marry you and promised to raise the baby as my own."

Aspen massaged her temple. Kurt's words vaguely rang true and stirred distant memories of a conversation, yet the details didn't quite break the surface. Had she been afraid of Jack's father physically? Afraid he'd try to take her son off the reservation?

"Did Aspen say the man was physical with her?" Dylan asked.

Kurt shrugged. "Not in so many words. But he wasn't Ute, and Aspen wanted to raise her son in the Ute way. So, when she went missing, I was afraid that the baby's father might have gone after her."

Dylan drummed his fingers on the table. "But if he wanted the baby, why leave him in the car?"

A shudder coursed through Aspen as she thought about her little boy in that car for God knew how long, cold and hungry and alone.

Kurt ran a hand over his forehead, sweating. "I don't know. Maybe he was married or a politician or something and didn't want anyone to know he was Jack's father."

Aspen twisted her hands in her lap. Something about that scenario seemed wrong. She might not remember much about her past, but she didn't think she would have gotten involved with a married man.

Her gaze met Dylan's and once again she lost herself in those blue eyes. Blue eyes like Jack's…

But that was impossible. She must be imagining things.

She'd only met Dylan at the shelter after the attack. And there were other blue-eyed men. She must have known someone in Las Vegas when she was working there. Another student maybe. Or a patron from the bar or casino.

"Anyway," Kurt gave Aspen another pleading look before turning to address Dylan. "She told me that if Jack's father came looking for her, she'd go to a women's shelter and disappear. That she'd adopt a new identity and start over somewhere else. That's when I decided to start looking at the shelters around the area. I thought if she was alive, that she might seek help from one."

"But I would never have left Jack," Aspen said.

"I didn't think you would," Kurt said. "That's why I figured you were hurt. Or that you might be coming back to get him. And when I found you at the Sisters of Mercy, I assumed you were making arrangements for a new life, and that you'd somehow get Jack and then take off."

Aspen tried to follow his logic. It made sense, but somehow still felt out of place.

"That doesn't explain why you didn't go up to the door and talk to the sisters," Dylan pointed out.

"Are you kidding?" Kurt asked. "Those women don't trust any man. They would never have let me near Aspen." He turned to her, his brown eyes darkening. "I swear, Aspen. I saw you a few times out in the courtyard, but you looked at me as if you didn't know me. That's when I knew something was really wrong. I only slipped into your room that night to talk to you, to see if I could help. To tell you that if you wanted to go somewhere else, that I'd take you and Jack."

"If that's true," Dylan said, "then you won't mind giving me your DNA." He laid a warrant on the table. "And then I'll need to search your house."

A flicker of anxiety registered on Kurt's face but he quickly masked it. "What are you looking for?"

"A gun," Dylan said. "And anything else that might prove you're lying."

"I don't own a gun," Kurt said gruffly.

Dylan cut him off, then ordered him to open wide while he swabbed the inside of his mouth.

DYLAN LEFT ASPEN, Jack and Emma with Bree again while he followed Lightfoot to his house to enforce the search warrant. Mentally, he sorted through the man's story, searching for the truth.

He wanted Lightfoot to be bad. Wanted to have a reason to get him away from Aspen.

But the man seemed to sincerely care for her. The fact that he'd offered to parent a child that he hadn't fathered was admirable.

Not that Dylan wouldn't do the same. He would.

But something else bothered him about Lightfoot. He said all the right things—maybe too right?

Or maybe you don't like him because he wants Aspen.

He wanted her, too.

Only wanting her had nothing to do with Jack. It had to do with the heavenly way she'd felt in his arms, in his bed. Her lips against his. Her body welcoming him inside hers. Her sultry voice whispering his name in the throes of passion.

"You're not going to find a weapon," Lightfoot said. "I'm a man of peace, not violence."

Dylan glared at him then proceeded inside the man's house, a simple wooden ranch that he assumed had been built by the WCA. The deer-hide rug, artwork and orange and yellow muted tones showed definite Native American influences.

It seemed Lightfoot and Aspen had a lot in common. Had she been in love with Lightfoot before the crash?

Worry gnawed at his gut. What if she hadn't told him about Jack because she didn't want him in her son's life? Lightfoot wasn't violent, claimed not to own a gun, worked for the WCA, whereas he was none of those things.

But he couldn't imagine Aspen leaving his bed in Vegas and jumping in bed with someone else so quickly.

Although she slept with you the first night you met.

But that was different. A hot, intense sexual chemistry had drawn them to each other immediately. And during that next week, the fire had only grown hotter.

He'd also learned more about her, found the woman beneath the exotic looks to be fascinating. Kind. Sincere. Intelligent.

And mesmerizing.

Lightfoot made a disgusted sound as Dylan rifled through his desk, but Dylan ignored him and searched the living area, closet, kitchen cabinets and pantry, then the bathroom before finally moving into the man's bedroom. A giant oak bed dominated the room with more Indian artwork. He grimaced as he checked beneath the mattress. Had Aspen ever been in this bed with Lightfoot? Moaned his name the way she'd moaned his when he'd made love to her?

Clenching his hands into fists and then unclenching them to regain control, he forced himself back to the job. He examined Lightfoot's dresser drawers, well aware Lightfoot watched with his arms folded angrily. The closet came next, and he pawed through the man's suede jacket, buffalo-skin coat, jeans and the top shelf.

Dammit. No weapon. Nothing suspicious.

He stalked to the other bedroom and searched it, as well, and again came up empty. Nothing to incriminate Lightfoot at all.

"Satisfied?" Lightfoot asked through clenched teeth.

Dylan offered him a stone-cold expression. "Just because it's not here doesn't mean you haven't had a gun and dumped it."

"You're looking at the wrong person," Lightfoot snarled. "I told you I would never hurt Aspen, and I meant it."

"You'd better not hurt her," Dylan said. "Because if you do, you'll answer to me personally."

Dylan headed to the door. He would keep digging. If Lightfoot had any ghosts in his closet, Dylan would expose every last one of them.

By the time he arrived back at Emma's, Miguel was there and Bree was gone. She'd received a call to check out some trouble on another part of the reservation. He hoped to hell it was a lead on Watts and Perkins. He wanted them in jail so Aspen would be safe from their evil clutches.

Aspen and Emma were playing with Jack on a pallet on the floor, and the baby laughed and cooed as Aspen told him a story about a game they played as children.

Miguel met him at the door, his look when he gazed at Emma one of a man in serious lust.

Dylan wondered if his own expression when he looked at Aspen was just as transparent.

"What did you find?" Miguel asked.

"Nothing." Dylan ran a hand over the scar on his chin.

"I heard Ryan suggest setting a trap by using Aspen as bait," Miguel said in a low voice. "Maybe you should consider it."

Rage seared Dylan, quick and raw. "Absolutely not."

Miguel shrugged. "It might be the only way to smoke out Perkins and Watts."

He narrowed his eyes at his brother, unable to believe what he'd suggested. "Would you use Emma as a trap?"

Miguel's face paled as he looked back at Emma. "No, I guess not. But I didn't realize you were in love with Aspen."

Dylan's chest clenched. He was attracted to her, wanted her back in his arms and in his bed. Hell, he wanted to take care of her and Jack whether Jack was his son or not. But he wasn't in love with Aspen.

Was he?

ASPEN HEARD THE PROTECTIVE tone in Dylan's voice when he'd refused to use her as a trap, and something warm, mellow and sweet bubbled inside her. And what had Miguel said—something about Dylan being in love with her?

Had she heard him correctly?

No…he must have been talking about loving Emma. While they were gone, more memories of Emma had returned, and she was glad that her cousin had found someone special to care for her.

She was also tired of being in the dark, living in fear while everyone tiptoed around her as if she'd lost her mind, not just her memories.

Dylan and Miguel had instantly hushed as soon as she approached them, driving home her point.

"What did you find at Kurt's?" she asked.

"Nothing." Dylan's intense eyes skated over her with a dark look that sent a tingle down her spine. "But he could have dumped a gun if he had one."

"You really don't trust him?" Aspen asked.

Dylan shrugged. "I'm not sure. I know I don't want you alone with him."

Aspen shivered, his possessive tone arousing a deep need in her to be held and protected by this man.

But instead of reaching for him, she hugged her arms around her waist. "I can't go on like this. Everyone keeping secrets from me, afraid to talk, afraid I'll break." She injected conviction into her voice. "I'm *not* going to break. I want to remember what happened. I don't like suspecting my friends or people on the reservation. And I hate not knowing who to trust."

Dylan studied her for a long moment, indecision in his eyes. "All right," he finally said. "But I've told you all we know for now."

"You haven't shown me pictures of the men you think I saw disposing of that woman's body."

"Do you think you're ready for that?" Dylan asked.

She nodded, summoning every ounce of courage she possessed. "Yes. Maybe seeing their faces will trigger my memory. Then I want you to take me to the scene of my accident."

A troubled expression darkened his eyes as if he was mentally debating what to do, but also a seed of hope surfaced when he gave a clipped nod. They'd reached an impasse and needed her help. She'd prove she was strong enough to handle it.

Because she and Jack couldn't live in fear forever.

THE WOMAN'S BIG BROWN EYES widened in horror as she realized his intent.

"Please don't kill me," she screeched. "I haven't done anything to you."

"I told you I need a place to hide out." He glanced around the modest little wooden bungalo. Not fancy but it would do. Just like the last place on the rez where he'd hidden.

But he had to keep moving. He couldn't get caught.

"You can stay here as long as you want," she whispered shakily as she tried to back toward the door. "I won't tell the police, I promise."

"Sorry, too late for that," he muttered.

He had to kill her. He couldn't leave any witnesses behind.

She tried to run, to escape, but he grabbed her by her long dark hair and jerked her back to him with a vicious yank. She screamed and flailed her puny arms, but he was stronger, and he slapped her across the face, then yanked out his knife and slashed her throat.

Blood spewed from her flesh and dripped down her pale neck, soaking her blouse in seconds.

Smiling, he dragged her limp body outside, weaving through the trees and brush, then tied rocks to her limbs and dumped her into the river.

Wiping sweat from his brow, he hiked back to the small cabin, went inside and scavenged through her refrigerator. A pizza, a six-pack of cold beer… His mouth watered. Damn, he'd hit the jackpot.

He'd kick back, get some rest, grab a shower and set up camp to watch for the right moment to kill Aspen Meadows.

Chapter Ten

"Are you sure you want to look at those photographs?" Dylan asked.

"Yes," Aspen said. "The sooner I recover my memories, the sooner we can put this mess behind us and move on with our lives."

Then he could leave the reservation and Aspen….

That thought sent his gut into a churning motion, but he had a job to do and he had to focus. Finding the person or persons after Aspen was the only way to keep her safe.

And he couldn't live with her death on his conscience.

Not like his little sister. He rubbed his thumb over his pocket where he kept Teresa's photo. God, she'd been so young and trusting, so full of life, her future looming ahead of her.

All lost in a second.

Hardening himself, he headed to the door. "Let me get the files from the car."

Wind slashed his cheeks as he stepped outside, his gaze immediately scanning the property to see if anyone was nearby. The night sounds of the reservation, of animals in the distance, surrounded him, the silence eerie as if danger lay nearby.

Hoping Aspen was truly strong enough to handle the photographs, he retrieved the files then carried them inside.

Emma was feeding Jack peaches, and Dylan couldn't help but grin as the sticky orange goop dribbled off his chin. But his smile died when Aspen gestured for him to spread the pictures on the coffee table.

The last thing he wanted to do was to hurt or traumatize Aspen more. But she seemed determined to push herself and face this gruesome task.

Which hopefully was a sign she was healing.

Miguel's cell phone rang, and he stepped outside to answer it.

Dylan removed the picture of Boyd Perkins, and Aspen's fingers trembled as she reached out and traced his bald head.

"Perkins is a hired gun," Dylan said.

She swallowed. "His eyes are ice-cold and mean."

"Goes with the territory. He works for a crime family." Dylan shifted. "There are two major crime families in the area, the Del Gardos and the Wayne family," Dylan explained. "We believe that Perkins was hired by Frank 'the Gun' Wayne's nephew, Nicky Wayne, who has taken over his uncle's organization. He ordered the hit on Vincent Del Gardo, the father of his rival Mob team. We also think that Perkins was supposed to locate fifty million dollars that it's been rumored Del Gardo hid from the government. Perkins used Sherman Watts—" he paused and added Watts's picture to the table "—to help him hide out on the reservation. Watts has a sheet for petty crimes, but up until we made the connection between him and Perkins, the police didn't think he was dangerous."

Aspen narrowed her eyes. "He does seem familiar."

"Watts lives on the reservation, so you might have seen him before that night."

Aspen's gaze drifted from Perkins to Watts, who had scraggly black hair that hung down beneath a black flat-brimmed hat.

"Watts is pretty much a loser. He loves booze and women." Dylan paused. "And Perkins probably offered to pay him to help him hide out."

Dylan removed a photo of Julie, his breath tightening. "This is Julie Grainger, the agent Perkins killed."

Aspen glanced up at him with a curious expression. She must have heard the pain in his voice because sympathy softened her eyes. "Her death was personal to you. You were in love with her?"

Dylan frowned and shook his head, studying her for any sign that she'd recognized the men or him. But only a sliver of fear glinted in her eyes. "No, nothing like that. We were friends, we worked together. She... was one of the good guys and didn't deserve to die so young."

She shivered, and he stroked her arm. "You don't have to do this, Aspen."

"No, I want to. I *need* to," she said emphatically. "Please take me to the crash site now." She jutted up her chin, making his heart ache for her.

He had wonderful, erotic memories of the two of them in bed. He wanted to make more of those memories, wanted to kiss her and alleviate the fear in her eyes.

But she was struggling to find her way back from the

dark. And if taking her to see the place where her ordeal had begun might help her, he'd do it.

Then and only then could she tell him the truth about Jack and what had happened to her.

His cell phone vibrated on his belt, and he grabbed it and checked the number. Bree. Hell, maybe she'd found Watts or Perkins.

He hastily punched the connect button. "Acevedo."

"Dylan, it's Bree. Listen, I went to check out that trouble on the reservation and think I may have found out where Perkins and Watts have been holding up."

"Where?"

"It's a small ranch that belongs to the Running Deer family. They were on vacation for a couple of weeks and just returned to find the place a mess, food and dishes piled up, dirt tracked in, beds slept in."

"Any sign of Watts or Perkins?"

"Looks like they left in a hurry. But there were cigarette butts and booze bottles so we should get some forensics. CSI's on its way, and I've called Sheriff Martinez to issue an APB in case they're still close by."

"Good," Dylan said. "Maybe we'll get lucky and catch them this time." He paused and glanced at Aspen. "Call me and let me know if you do. I want to be there for the questioning."

Miguel had stepped outside but strode back in, his expression strained.

Dylan disconnected the call, his pulse racing.

Miguel had bad news.

ASPEN THUMBED HER FINGERS through the tangled strands of her hair. "Did they find them?"

Miguel looked confused, so Dylan explained about

Bree's call. "She thinks they may be close so she and Patrick are searching the rez near the Running Deer house."

"I hope to hell they find them," Miguel muttered.

Emma returned from the bedroom where she'd put Jack down for a nap. "What's going on?"

Miguel relayed the latest on Perkins and Watts. "Dylan, I just talked to the ME," Miguel said. "Maybe we should step outside."

"No," Aspen said. "Emma and I are a part of this. We deserve to know everything that's going on."

Dylan gave a reluctant nod, and Miguel shifted, looking uncomfortable. "It's about a past case. Frank Turnbull, the serial killer who killed all those Ute girls last year." He gestured toward Dylan. "Dylan tracked him down and arrested him. He's been in jail for murder for the past few months."

Aspen frowned, something about the case nagging at her. The Ute women had had their throats slashed. "What happened?"

"He was being transferred to APX Florence, and his bus crashed and burned," Dylan interjected, then turned to Miguel. "Do they have a positive ID?"

Miguel sighed. "The ME said they found a partial bridge plate that belonged to Turnbull. Matched it to Turnbull's dental records. But they're still working on the bones."

Dylan shifted on the balls of his feet. "That's good but not conclusive. After I drive Aspen to the crash site, I'm going to study his prison correspondence. We can't let down our guard until we verify that he's dead." And if he was, a copycat had surfaced. Maybe Turnbull had a fan who'd decided to imitate him.

Or what if he'd had an accomplice? Some serial killers worked in pairs. They'd considered that theory before but hadn't found any evidence to support it.

He glanced at Emma. "Do you mind watching Jack while I drive Aspen?"

"Of course not," Emma said softly. "I'll be glad to take care of him anytime you need."

Dylan placed a hand at Aspen's waist. "Are you ready?"

Aspen inhaled, determined to push forward. "Yes, let's go."

He ushered her to the car, scanning the property as they climbed in and drove off the reservation. Aspen sat in silence, her hands knotted, her gaze focused on the rugged terrain, steep slopes, ridges and brush. The scenery felt as familiar as her name had, and her love of the land returned, welcoming her home. Although it was May, in the distance, snow still capped the mountaintops, and a cool wind rattled the windowpanes, causing goose bumps to scatter along her arms.

The moon struggled to break through dark storm clouds that hovered above like winter ghosts taunting her with the threat of bad weather, the eerie sounds of the isolated area near the river echoing in the night.

Dylan bumped over rocky, dirt-packed ground and steered the vehicle toward an isolated area near the river, tucked in the shadows of the trees and foliage standing guard over the water rushing below.

He pointed toward a large tree across the way, its gnarled branches sweeping down as if to enfold them within its spidery dark hold.

She suddenly felt Dylan's hand slide over hers, the warmth of his body enveloping her as if he held her in his arms, as if he would keep the danger at bay.

"Aspen?"

"I'm ready," she said, mustering her courage and reaching for the door.

He opened his side and exited, then met her in front of the car. Her body trembled but she forced her feet forward until she stood in front of the tree. Even in the dark, she saw paint marks embedded in the bark that had been damaged from the impact of her car.

"This is where your car was found," Dylan said in a quiet but gravely voice.

An image of her red sedan flashed back then terror consumed her as snippets of that night returned. But other memories rushed to the forefront.

She was nine months pregnant, walking along the river when she'd spotted two men in the distance. One with scraggly black hair and a black hat, the other bald. They were dragging something.

Dear God, a body.

Her voice caught on a scream, and the men turned, searching through the trees looking for the source of the sound. A pain shot through her stomach, and she clutched her belly, a contraction hitting her full force. She leaned against a tree trunk and breathed through the squeezing torture, hiding behind the foliage. She had to get of there, get away.

If they'd killed someone, they'd probably kill her, too.

And her baby—she had to protect her child.

The pain slowly subsided, and she took off running, weaving through the brush and branches, checking over her shoulder to make sure they weren't behind her. By the time she staggered to her car, she was shaking and panting. She clutched the door handle, ripped it open and collapsed inside as another contraction seized her.

She leaned against the steering wheel, struggling to breathe through it, her thoughts racing. She should call the police, have them check for the body. Tell them what she'd seen.

But her vision blurred, and the events lost focus. What if it hadn't been a body? Maybe the men had shot a deer or elk...

And if she called the police, what if the men tracked her down and hurt her baby?

No...they'd be safer if she stayed quiet. Another pain caught her in its clutches, and she glanced at her watch. Only two minutes since the last contraction.

She had to make it to the midwife to help her deliver the baby....

"Aspen, are you all right?" A gentle hand stroked her back, soothing her.

She nodded, perspiration beading on her neck. "Yes, I remember seeing two men dragging a body. But I was scared...and having contractions." She heaved for a breath. "So I ran. I had to protect the baby."

"Of course you did," he said quietly. "Then what happened? Did the men see you?"

She clutched at him for support. "I wasn't sure. But later, after Jack was born, I heard about that agent's body being found. I knew then that I'd witnessed a crime..." Tears laced her voice. "I'm sorry, Dylan. I should have come forward sooner."

"You had a child to protect," he said with more understanding than she deserved.

He massaged her shoulders. "What happened after that?"

She closed her eyes, allowing the memories to come now. They were flooding her mind, rushing at her like a dam had broken.

She'd driven back to the scene, hoping to trigger details about the men to tell the police. But the men appeared out of nowhere as if they'd been watching for her.

She ran again, and quickly strapped Jack into the car seat. She had to get to the police.

Frantically, she cranked the engine, pressed the gas and tore down the graveled road. But a moment later, a dark car raced up on her tail and chased her off the road. Jack was screaming in the back, and she tried to soothe him with her voice, but fear clogged her throat, and she cried out as the car slammed into her and sent her flying into the tree. Tires had squealed, glass shattering, metal crunching, but the sound of Jack's distress wrenched her heart.

Dear God, her baby couldn't die…

With that choking thought, she'd fought her way past the air bag and ripped off her seat belt, desperate to reach him and make sure he was safe.

But rough, big hands dragged her from the car, yanking her by the hair. A fist slammed into her head and the ground clawed at her arms and legs. She screamed and kicked but another blow to her head made her legs buckle and the world spin into darkness.

By the time she fought through the nausea and the pull of unconsciousness, she was falling, falling, falling…

Through the dark space and into the icy water, her body slammed against the jagged rocks, the cold enveloping her until she was numb and knew she was going to die.

"Aspen?"

She didn't realize she was standing on the precipice of the ridge with the river raging below until Dylan suddenly jerked her back.

She was shaking and crying, the terror all too real as if she'd just been submerged into the frigid river again.

"Shh, baby, I'm here," Dylan whispered. "You're safe."

A warmth engulfed her as Dylan pulled her into his arms, and she burrowed against him, taking solace in his embrace and voice.

"Aspen, honey, are you all right?"

She nodded against him, and he literally felt her grappling for a breath, and sensed the terror in her trembling body.

"It's over now," he murmured into her hair. "I won't let them hurt you again."

"I was so scared for Jack," she whispered hoarsely. "They talked about killing him, but then decided he'd probably die in the cold anyway."

Dylan muttered a curse. Damn bastards would pay for leaving an innocent little baby alone to face the brutal winter elements.

"Jack's safe now, too," he whispered. "I promise they'll never harm either one of you again."

She turned teary eyes up to him, her lip quivering. "Why do you care so much? Why are you here protecting me and Jack?"

It's my job, he wanted to say. But she'd said she wanted the truth, not to be left in the dark. And, dammit, she was in his arms and he wanted to make her remember the time they'd spent together.

That her safety meant much more to him than any damn case.

He tucked a strand of her hair behind her ear, soaking up her features like a starving man. "Because I do care," he said quietly.

Her eyes searched his and for a moment, he thought he saw a flicker of recognition dawn in her eyes as if she remembered him. Her breath caught, her heart beating against his, and his body hardened, aching with the need to touch her, to strip her and join his body with hers.

To remind them both that she had survived.

Unable to resist, he lowered his mouth and pressed his lips to hers. Tentative at first. Testing. Tasting. Begging for her to recall what they'd shared. To invite him to explore her.

To take her the way he once had.

She moaned and threaded her fingers in his hair, all the invitation he needed to deepen the kiss. She opened her mouth, playing her own tongue along his, sending heat spiraling through him in erotic, torturous waves.

His hands slid lower, stroking her shoulders, her back, the soft column of her spine until he pulled her deeper into his embrace, her heat against his own, his thighs cradling her when her legs threatened to give way.

She moaned, the sultry sound indicating she liked the feel of his kiss, and that she wanted more. She clung to him, her hands needy and frenzied as she traced them over his chest and his arms.

Heat seared him, hunger bolting through his body at lightning speed.

Just like it had the first time he'd met her.

But suddenly a shot pinged through the air, whizzing next to his head. Aspen screamed, and he shoved her to the ground behind a large rock, shielding her with his body as he removed his gun and searched for the shooter in the dark.

HE CROUCHED ON HIS KNEES, then crawled along the rocky embankment, his gun trained on Acevedo. He had to take the man out. Or at least impair him until he could get to the woman.

She was the one he wanted now.

But he'd be more than happy to kill the agent, too.

First, though, he had to make the woman suffer....

Chapter Eleven

Dylan cursed, scanning the woods as he grabbed Aspen's hand and led her through the trees toward the car.

Another shot grazed by her head, and she screamed as he jerked sideways to dodge the bullet. It hit the side of the car, and Dylan dragged her behind the rear bumper for cover.

Crouching down, he coaxed her to the passenger side and opened the door. "Get in and stay down."

She crawled into the car, burying her head beneath her arms. He shut the door, then circled back, searching for the shooter. A shadow of a man appeared in the distance, and he contemplated chasing him down.

He was tired of being the target.

But Aspen was in the car and he had to protect her. If this was Perkins and Watts, they might have divided up, might be watching, hoping to separate them so they could get to her.

Another shot hit the dirt beside him, and he inched around the back bumper to the driver's side, staying crouched and hiding behind the door as he opened it. Then he slid inside, turned the key and backed down the graveled drive, flooring the gas as another bullet spun toward them.

As he flew onto the highway, he reached over and stroked Aspen's hair, hating the way her body trembled. They had to find Watts and Perkins. She didn't deserve to live in fear, to have to look over her shoulder.

He grabbed his cell phone and called Sheriff Martinez. "Patrick, it's Dylan Acevedo. A shooter just fired at us from the site where we found Aspen's car."

Patrick hissed. "I'll send some units to the area immediately."

"Thanks. I'll stop by the crime lab and dig out the bullet in the car and leave it for ballistics," Dylan said.

He disconnected the call, but kept glancing over his shoulder as he raced away, relaxing only slightly when he didn't spot anyone behind them.

Finally he told Aspen he thought they were safe, and she crawled into the seat and strapped on her seat belt. "We have to do something," she said in a shaky voice. "I can't keep running."

"We're doing everything we can," Dylan said, although frustration hardened his voice.

"Are you?" Aspen asked.

He frowned at her. "What's that supposed to mean?"

"I heard you talking to Miguel. You said that one of the agents suggested you use me as bait to trap Watts and Perkins."

Emotions pummeled him. "Absolutely not."

She brushed a strand of hair from her cheek. "Why not? I witnessed those men dump the woman's body. I remember them coming after me. I want to testify against them."

"I said no."

Aspen's eyes widened. "I don't understand. They're after me anyway, so why not take the proactive route and set them up?"

"Because they could kill you," Dylan said through clenched teeth.

"But you'll be there to protect me," Aspen argued.

"And what if I can't?" His tone turned razor sharp, the adrenaline from their earlier attack firing his temper. "What if I fail? I couldn't live with that...."

An odd look flickered in her eyes and she suddenly touched her lips. Was she remembering the kiss, the kiss that he'd wanted and had almost taken too far?

The kiss that had distracted him so that the shooter had gotten close enough to nearly kill them.

ASPEN TOUCHED HER LIPS, something about their conversation striking a familiar chord of recognition as if they'd had this discussion before.

His voice had cracked, almost as if protecting her was something more than a case to him, something *personal.*

But that was impossible...wasn't it?

Except that that kiss had stirred feelings inside her. Feelings of hunger and desire and need.

Feelings that disturbed her because they ran deeper than they should for someone she'd just met. Feelings that felt familiar.

"Dylan?"

His jaw was clenched, his hands wrapped around the steering wheel in a white-knuckled grip. "I'm sorry," he muttered. "I can't take that chance."

"But it makes sense, and it may be the only way—"

"No. I care about you, dammit."

Her breath caught in her chest. He'd said that before. "What?"

He growled in his throat and ran a hand through his hair, then steered the car off the road and pulled behind a boulder as if to hide them in case someone was following. Then he turned to her, his blue eyes glittering with emotions she couldn't define.

His breathing sounded choppy in the ensuing silence. Then he clenched and unclenched his fists as if in a silent debate. "God, I'm not supposed to do this."

Aspen touched his arm, automatically feeling his strength seep into her, his heat warming her insides and sparking a fire low in her belly. "You're not supposed to do what?"

"I'm not supposed to push you. The doctor said to let you remember on your own."

"But I'm starting to," she whispered. "And I told you before I don't want to be left in the dark."

His gaze probed her. "But you didn't remember me when I kissed you, did you?"

"We knew each other before," she said in a low voice, then pressed her fingers to her mouth. "It's true, isn't it? That's why it felt so…familiar."

He gave a clipped nod, then reached for her arms and gently held her. "Yes, we knew each other. We met last year in Vegas right after I arrested the Ute serial killer."

"That's why I recognized the name Turnbull."

"Probably, although the case was major news. But we talked about it that first night." He sighed, looking tired and defeated. "I was upset. All those women had died, and for weeks I'd been looking at gruesome photos of

Turnbull's murder victims, then I walked into that bar, and saw you and..."

"And what?" Aspen asked.

"And you were so damn beautiful that I watched you all night, then walked you to your apartment and stayed."

A fleeting memory tickled her conscience. Her in Dylan's arms, kissing, touching...stripping and falling into bed. "The first night?"

"Yes," he said, his voice cracking slightly. "We spent the week together, Aspen. A week in bed, making love to each other."

His words evoked erotic memories that aroused her and made her tingly inside. The first time she'd touched him at the shelter, she'd felt an electric chemistry between them. But she'd chalked her reaction up to fear.

Had thought she was drawn to him because he promised protection when she was grappling to plow her way back to the world she'd lost.

Another thought struck her. She'd wondered about Jack's bright blue eyes...

"I probably shouldn't have told you," he murmured in a tortured voice.

"No, I'm glad you did." Aspen gripped his hand. "Tell me what happened next."

Dylan's look turned pained, but he cradled her hand between his. "I was called away on an undercover assignment, so we parted. You told me your plans to return to the reservation to teach, and you obviously followed through."

Disappointment ballooned in her chest. "You're saying that we had a fling? A meaningless affair?"

Tension stretched between them then he finally

sighed heavily. "I thought my job would get in the way," he finally said. "That you'd be safer without me in your life. Then Julie was murdered and you went missing, and I had to come here to find out who killed Julie." His voice cracked. "And I had to find you, to know if you were all right."

The pain and worry in his voice sounded far too real for her to believe that he hadn't cared. Still, she didn't know how to react. Because the truth was that he'd walked away without contacting her until the case had brought him back into her life again.

And had she just let him leave? Had he meant more to her than a one-week affair?

She struggled to tamp down the hurt eating at her and glanced at the road, suddenly anxious to set the trap, and catch the men after her.

She couldn't become too needy. Couldn't fall for a man who could walk away from her the way he had. She had a child to think of. Her irresponsible days were over, had ended with Jack's birth.

Another memory surfaced—this one of her mother. When Aspen's father had deserted her before she was born, her mother had guarded her personal life. She hadn't paraded a sea of men into their house because she hadn't wanted Aspen to get too attached. To call a stranger daddy then have him walk out on her.

Aspen had to safeguard her son the same way.

DYLAN KNEW HE'D ADMITTED TOO much, but his emotions were bouncing all over the place.

Dammit, she could have died back there, and it would have been his fault. His hand automatically went to his pocket and he felt the folded edges of Teresa's picture taunting him.

Angry with himself, he started the car, checked the road, grateful not to detect a car hunting them down, then headed in to Kenner City to the crime lab.

"Dylan, please," Aspen said. "Call the other agents and let's set a trap. It may be the only way you can catch Boyd Perkins and Sherman Watts. I won't let Jack grow up living in fear."

"I don't want that, either," he said gruffly. Resigned, he phoned Tom and asked him to meet him at the crime lab.

Tension thrummed between them, questions left unspoken. He felt raw, exposed as if he'd finally confessed that she meant more to him than just a job, and it still hurt to know that she had no memory of the incredible week they'd shared.

That he still wanted her and she might not feel the same way.

A stiff wind battered the car as he crossed into the city and parked at the annex building. Senses alert, he scanned the outside of the building, then guided Aspen inside to the third-floor crime lab.

Tom met them at the door to the conference room, and Ava and Callie stepped inside, along with Bart Flemming. He introduced them to Aspen, then explained about the shooting, and Callie asked Jerry to dig the bullets from the rental car to compare to the others.

"We're glad you're safe," Callie said.

The others murmured agreement, and everyone settled into seats around the conference table.

"I'm still working on processing the evidence Bree and Patrick sent over from the Running Deer house,"

Ava said. "I identified Perkins's and Watts's prints inside, which confirms they were there."

"So they still are on the reservation?" Dylan said.

Callie shrugged. "As of a couple of days ago, it looks that way."

Bart piped up. "Well, I have something, too. Not to do with Perkins and Watts, but on Kurt Lightfoot."

Dylan's interest was piqued. "What did you find?"

"He works for the WCA and has done a lot of work for the Ute community, but I dug further into some of the contract jobs and suppliers and found something interesting." He paused. "There may be a link between him and the Wayne family."

"You mean, he's taking money for the WCA to help the reservation?" Aspen asked.

"Maybe."

Dylan chewed over that idea. "In exchange for what?"

Bart raised a hand. "I'm still looking."

"Maybe we should bring him in for questioning," Dylan suggested.

Bart tapped his pencil on the desk. "Give me another day or two and I may have something more definitive."

Dylan nodded and glanced at Aspen, his own need and hunger for Aspen warring with his logic. Setting a trap would definitely be the fastest way to smoke out their perps, but putting Aspen's life in more danger terrified him.

But he didn't have to speak up. Aspen did.

"We visited the crime scene earlier, and I remembered seeing Boyd Perkins and Sherman Watts dumping that woman's body." She paused, a strained look in her eyes. "I should have come forward immediately, but I was afraid," she admitted. "And at first, I wasn't certain what I'd seen. Then when I heard about a woman's body being found on the reservation, I knew I'd witnessed a crime."

Dylan spoke up, determined to cut her some slack. "Aspen was pregnant and went into labor," he said. "But later she decided to come forward, then Watts and Perkins recognized her. That's when they chased her down and she crashed into the tree."

"They tried to strangle me, then threw me in the river," Aspen said in a haunted voice.

"You guys know the rest," Dylan said.

Aspen cleared her throat. "I'm ready to testify. I overheard Miguel and Dylan talking about setting the trap for Perkins and Watts," Aspen said. "And I think it's a good idea. These men belong behind bars."

Dead silence met her declaration. Ryan and Callie shifted, then nervous glances crisscrossed the room between the agents and forensics specialists.

Finally Ben Parrish spoke up. "I think that's a smart move."

"I can contact the press immediately and let them know we have a witness and that Aspen is ready to testify," Ryan said.

Dylan planted a fist on the table. "We'll only agree to do this if I can move Aspen and her son to a safe house."

Murmurs of agreement rumbled through the room, along with excitement that they might finally be taking action.

As if in agreement, everyone stood. "I'll get back to processing the evidence," Ava said.

"And I'll finish that background check on Lightfoot," Flemming added.

Callie cleared her throat. "Dylan. Can I see you in my office for a second?"

Dylan's gaze met Aspen's, an intense heat simmering between them, his heart pounding so loudly at the thought of Aspen being used as bait that her words barely registered.

Then he jerked himself back to work. "Of course." He glanced at Aspen. "I'll be right back."

He followed Callie into her office, shoulders tightening with tension.

Did she have the results of the paternity test?

Was Jack his son, or would he learn that another man had found his way into her bed and given her a child?

Chapter Twelve

Dylan braced himself as he entered Callie's office. "What is it?" he asked without preamble.

She raised a brow with a smirk. "You always are to the point, Acevedo." She indicated a folder on her desk. "The test results you asked for are in."

"Hell, Callie, you enjoy torturing a guy?"

She threw her head back and laughed. "No. But I'm not sure you want to hear this news. I guess that depends on how you feel about Aspen Meadows."

"She's just a case."

"Right."

He steeled himself against an outward reaction, resorting to the training he'd relied on to keep him stable and on task. "It doesn't matter. I just need the truth. Jack's paternity could prove to be a lead…or not."

"It's not," she said slyly.

A seed of hope slivered through him, and he jerked up the file, flipped it open and scanned the lab report.

Jack was his son.

The paternity test proved it beyond a shadow of a doubt.

A slow smile spread on his face as his breath whooshed

out. He stumbled slightly, the exhilaration of knowing he shared a child with Aspen, that he'd known when he'd held him, drumming through his chest.

Emotions he hadn't expected to feel overpowered him. The thrill of knowing that his legacy would live on, that the time he'd spent with Aspen had been so strong that they'd produced a beautiful little boy with their physical bond.

On the heels of that joy, anger followed, the realization that he'd missed the first few months of his son's life.

That Aspen hadn't contacted him to inform him that he had a son.

And that Jack didn't have his name.

Lightfoot's comment that she'd claimed she was afraid of the baby's father taunted him. Why would Aspen have been afraid of him?

He gripped the folder with an iron fist and turned to go to Aspen and confront her.

But Callie planted herself in front of the door. "I know you're upset," she said in a low voice. "But stop and remember the situation, Dylan, and the doctor's warning about pushing Aspen too far."

"This is different," he ground out through the lump in his throat.

"No, it's not," she said gently. "She's still a witness in our protection. And if you upset her, she could run. That would only endanger her more."

Callie's words made nervous sweat explode above his brow, and he dropped into the chair by her desk and lowered his head into his hands. She was right.

But, dammit, he didn't like it.

Still, the last thing he wanted was to see the mother of his son hurt.

Or killed because he'd gone half-cocked, scared her, and sent her running into the night, vulnerable and at the hands of the very men he'd vowed to protect her from.

ASPEN STIFFENED as Dylan entered the conference room. His body language indicated something between them had changed. An air of fury radiated off of him that sent a chill through her.

Dylan rapped his knuckles on the table to get everyone's attention. "Let's work on the details of the trap. First, the press will leak the news that Aspen recovered her memory and is ready to testify." He angled his head toward her. "But you and Jack both remain under protective custody at all times. There will be no personal contact with anyone, not Emma or the other friends you made on the reservation. And when we stop by to pick up Jack, if Lightfoot comes by, we give nothing away."

Aspen nodded, although the thought of breaking off contact with Emma, the one family member she had left disturbed her. She'd felt isolated at the women's shelter in Mexican Hat. Now she'd be totally under Dylan's thumb.

And although she'd sensed different vibes coming from him—sometimes an intense heat that obviously had begun the year before—anger now tightened his jaw and hardened his words.

"Do you understand, Aspen?" he asked. "No contact with anyone. It's just you and me and Jack."

She twined her fingers together. "How long will we be...contained?" She'd almost said *imprisoned.*

His broad shoulders shrugged but his expression

didn't soften. "Until Perkins and Watts are in custody, and I'm certain you're safe."

Her hesitation seemed to irritate him more. "Aspen?"

"Yes," she said, although nerves tinged her voice. Knowing that she and Dylan shared a past, that they'd slept together, made the thought of being totally alone with him for days—or weeks—almost shatter her resolve to set the trap.

But she looked into his eyes and a memory surfaced—Dylan tenderly holding her, caressing her, trailing kisses down her neck and breasts. His hands roaming over her, teasing, exploring, drawing an erotic response from her nerve endings until she begged for more.

Was she always such a wanton lover, or had she only been that way in his arms?

DYLAN COULD BARELY LOOK AT Aspen. He wanted to shake her and make her tell him the truth about Jack.

He wanted to kiss her until she melted in his arms and welcomed him into his son's life.

And into hers.

But how would that work? He still had a dangerous job which would put her and Jack in jeopardy.

His cell phone rang, and he checked the number. Sheriff Martinez. He connected the call. "Acevedo."

"Dylan, you guys need to get over here. Bree and I found a body."

"Perkins or Watts?"

"No, it's a woman's. I've already called the ME."

An uneasy feeling clutched Dylan's chest. "I'll be right there."

He gave him the coordinates, and disconnected the call, then relayed the gist of the conversation to the others. "I'll stop and check it out on the way back to Aspen's to pick up her things for the safe house."

Ava and Callie jumped into motion to retrieve their crime scene kits to go to the scene.

Ben threw up a hand. "I'll set up the safe house in Mesa Verde."

"Thanks." Dylan took Aspen's elbow and guided her to the door. "Let's go."

"What's wrong?" Aspen asked.

"Other than a girl is dead and we're using you as bait for a killer?"

"I'm sorry," Aspen said in a contrite voice. "I just thought there was something else disturbing you."

He gritted his teeth to keep from asking about Jack.

The fact that Martinez had specifically requested him worried him, too.

The wind whipped the car as they climbed in, the windowpanes rattling as they drove across the reservation. Dylan's nerves were on edge as he constantly scanned the deserted roads and hiding spots for another attacker or car following them.

He parked on the ridge by Martinez's police car, and Callie and Ava parked beside him, climbing out with their kits in hand.

He pressed a hand on Aspen's shoulder. "Stay here and keep the doors locked. If anything happens, honk the horn and I'll be here in a second."

"I could go with you," Aspen offered.

Not knowing what he would find or the condition of the woman's body, he shook his head. "No. This is official police work. The fewer people contaminating the scene, the better."

She nodded in understanding, and he climbed out and punched the lock button before heading down the embankment to where Martinez and Bree were waiting. Bree met him at the bottom of the hill.

The scent of the murky water, vegetation and death swirled in the breeze as he approached the river where Martinez stood beside the local medical examiner. Dr. Pruitt, a fortysomething, gray-haired man with a cleft chin, was bent over the body, examining it.

Dylan braced himself to view another dead female body as he stepped closer. Martinez angled his head and moved to the side to give him a better view and Dylan's stomach churned.

Her hair was matted, skin pale white with fish and bug bites, her throat slashed from ear to ear.

"How long has she been dead?" Martinez asked.

"A day at least, but it's hard to tell with the decomp. The temperature of the water helped preserve her but the fish…" He shook his head. "Damn son of a bitch tied her down so she'd sink. But a couple of the knots slipped loose and she floated to the top. Some rafters found her caught between some rocks."

"You questioned them?" Dylan asked.

Bree spoke up. "Yeah, it was a couple of teenagers. They were pretty freaked out. I called their parents and they already took them home."

"Cause of death?" Martinez asked.

The medical examiner lifted the woman's head slightly, and Dylan noted the slash mark on her neck. A slash mark that looked sickeningly familiar.

"She has a bruise on the back of her head and several on her body, but basically, her throat was slashed and she bled out. Forensics may be able to tell us more about the kind of knife the killer used."

The rope tied to the woman's wrist made bile rise to Dylan's throat.

At the end of the rope, he saw the chunk of thunderwood.

Dylan ground his teeth together. Callie muttered something under her breath, and Ava gave a small gasp.

"What do you think?" Martinez asked Dylan.

Dylan's throat thickened with fear. "You know what I think."

"It could be a copycat," Callie suggested.

Dylan met her gaze. "I know. Or Turnbull could have survived that crash and have started all over again."

"But it doesn't quite fit Turnbull's MO," Ava said. "Turnbull left his victims out in the open for us to find as if he was gloating about it. This time the body was tied and dumped in the river so we wouldn't find her."

Dylan stewed over that point. "Maybe he wasn't ready to let us know he'd survived the accident."

"Or Watts and Perkins did it and used the thunderwood to throw us off," Ava suggested.

"Find out who she is," Dylan said. "I'll phone Warden Fernandez to alert him of our suspicions." He'd also see if he'd sent over Turnbull's prison correspondence and take it with him to the safe house. Then he'd review it himself to see if Turnbull had orchestrated an escape or if they were dealing with a copycat.

Because this girl wouldn't be his last victim.

And the fact that he'd found a piece of thunderwood

on Aspen's doorstep meant that the man would be coming for her.

Dylan had to be ready when he did. If he laid one hand on Aspen, he'd forget prison this time.

He'd kill the son of a bitch even if he had to go to prison himself afterwards.

THE TENSION IN THE CAR as they drove back to Emma's made Aspen queasy. She'd returned home again, and now she had to leave her house, her cousin, everything behind. Worse, she had no idea how long she'd be gone.

Only that Dylan was going to be with her around the clock.

Under other circumstances, spending time with the sexy, handsome agent might be pleasant.

His gaze slid over her and her body tingled as she remembered the heated kiss earlier. She amended her thoughts. It wouldn't just be pleasant, it would be downright fun.

They might explore where that kiss could lead and recreate the passionate week he'd claimed they'd spent together when they'd first met.

He parked at Emma's and her heart sputtered with excitement at the thought of seeing her son again. How could she have forgotten him all those weeks? He was so much a part of her that she'd missed him the past few hours.

As soon as they entered, she smelled the scent of homemade stew and spicy jalapeno corn bread, and her stomach growled. Emma greeted her with a hug and Miguel stepped outside with Dylan.

"How did it go?" Emma asked.

Aspen explained that her memory had returned, and about the trap they planned to set for Perkins and Watts.

Emma's eyes widened in horror. "That sounds dangerous."

Aspen shrugged off her concern. "Dylan and Jack and I are moving to a safe house. Other agents will watch my house and if Perkins or Watts appear, they'll catch them. Then the danger will be over and Jack and I will be safe."

Dylan and Miguel came in wearing scowls. "You told Emma about the plan?" Dylan asked.

She nodded.

Miguel moved to stand beside Emma, a protective gleam in his eyes. "Did she tell you that Frank Turnbull may have escaped? That they found a Ute woman killed with the same MO?"

Emma leaned one hand against the table edge with a shudder, and Miguel took her in his arms. "That means you don't go anywhere without me, *Loca Linda*."

Emma nodded. "Don't worry. I don't intend to."

"I phoned the ME who's been analyzing the bodies from the prison bus crash and told him to put a rush on those bones," Dylan said. "If Turnbull has escaped, we need to put out the word. And if we have a copycat, we need to do the same."

Dylan's gaze met Aspen's. Fear glittered in his eyes for a brief second before he masked it.

Did he have reason to think that Frank Turnbull might come after her?

THE UTE SLICER WAS LEGENDARY. Had earned fame and a reputation that would follow him into eternity.

He'd smiled as he'd watched from the top of the ridge as the Feds and police recovered the woman's body. He hadn't expected them to find her so soon, but hell, maybe this was a good thing.

The cops would be sweating. Sympathizing with the victim. Trying to figure out who he was.

While he was one step ahead of them.

The memory of slicing the woman's throat made his body go hard, and he mentally envisioned the knife piercing the girl's delicate flesh, then the blood gurgling and flowing down his hands.

The whites of her eyes had turned stark with terror when she realized her death was imminent.

Hell, yeah, it had been a rush he hadn't felt in a long damn time.

Let them shake in their shoes and stew for a while now. Try to figure out if Turnbull had survived or if a copycat had surfaced to mimic the man's crimes.

He held the knife up to the moonlight, the sharp blade glinting.

Meanwhile, life for some went on.

But for others, it was time to say a final goodbye.

Chapter Thirteen

"Go pack," Dylan said as soon as they entered Aspen's house. "I want us to get out of here before the evening news airs."

Aspen cradled Jack to her as if he was afraid to release him. "He needs changing before we go."

"I'll take care of it," Dylan said. "Get your things together, then you can pack whatever we'll need for the baby." He hesitated, sensing her distress and reluctance to leave her home when she'd just found her way back. "Unless you've changed your mind." He grabbed her arm. "If you have, it's okay. I'll call off the whole damn plan."

She kissed Jack's forehead, her grip around the baby tightening as if she didn't want to let him go, but resignation lit her eyes and she eased Jack into his arms. "No. Those men have to be caught and put away."

He gently embraced the little boy, Jack's arms and legs kicking playfully. Aspen stroked the baby's cheek, then turned and rushed into her room.

Dylan released the pent up feelings he'd been holding in ever since Callie had given him the results of the paternity tests. Unbidden, moisture pricked his eyes as he pulled the blanket away from his son's face and gazed into his eyes.

His own blue eyes.

"My God, you are amazing," he whispered hoarsely. "You are my little *mijo,* my son, and I will never leave you now."

Jack grabbed his finger and curled his fist around it as if he understood.

Dylan's heart swelled with love. There was no way he could walk away from his baby or Aspen.

He'd die before he let anyone hurt them again.

ASPEN BLINKED BACK TEARS as they left her house. Almost desperately she glanced back, memorizing the details of it as if she might forget where she lived once again.

"We're not going far," Dylan said, giving her hand a squeeze as if he sensed her distress. "We'll still be in Mesa Verde country."

Still among her people. She took some solace in that.

She squeezed his hand in return, grateful to know that he wouldn't leave her until they'd caught the men after her.

But then he would move on.

That realization sent an ache through her, an emptiness that reminded her of how lonely she'd felt the last few weeks when she'd been isolated and scared and had no one to turn to.

Jack gurgled from the back, and she turned sideways to comfort him. "It's okay, sweet one, we're just taking a little trip. An adventure."

Dylan gave her an odd look. "That was what my parents used to call it when we went on vacation."

She relaxed slightly. "Tell me about your family."

A wistful look passed across his face as he steered them toward Cortez. "My family comes from a long line of farmers who grew potatoes and alfalfa in the San Luis Valley. My parents were the first ones to go to college." A proud smile curved his mouth. "Papa is an attorney. He calls himself King Pro Bono. And Mama is an artist and teacher at Adams State College in Alamosa."

"You have other siblings?"

He nodded, although the scar at his chin twitched. "You met Miguel. I also have another brother and sister who are married with kids. And then there was Teresa." His tone lowered a decibel. "She died in a drive-by shooting when she was a teenager."

His story tapped at her memory banks as if he'd shared it before. "I'm sorry. That must have been horrible for your family."

He made a pained noise deep in his throat. "I was standing right there, only a few feet away. It should have been me."

She heard the agony in his voice, the guilt. "Her death inspired you to go into police work?"

He gave a self-deprecating laugh. "In a roundabout way." He sighed and rammed his hand through his hair, spiking the dark strands. "I was enraged, went looking for revenge. My father, Papa, was working the courts, my mother grieving. It was a rough time for all of us."

"And Miguel?"

"He was a damn altar boy. The smart, scientific one where I was the troublemaker."

"I'm sure that's not true."

"Oh, it was," he said with conviction. "Miguel toyed with being a priest. But he got shot defending his girlfriend and had a near-death experience. That changed him, and he decided to go into forensics and study medicine. He claimed that's what saved him. Although my mother always insisted that it wasn't the medical procedures that saved him but the healing soil of El Santuario de Chimayo and prayer."

"I think I'd like your mother," Aspen said softly.

A sultry smile softened his eyes as he turned to look at her. "You would. And I know she'd like you."

Aspen's heart melted at his words. His family sounded loving, honorable, spiritual, and reminded her of her own mother, and the role model she wanted to be for her son.

But what about a father or male figure for Jack to identify with?

She had managed without one. But was it different for a boy? Did he need a man in his life?

ASPEN'S QUESTIONS ABOUT HIS family triggered bitter-sweet memories. The family trips, the camping, the cookouts, the normal childhood fights between siblings.

The empty hole Teresa's death had created.

The Christmas ornament they still hung on the tree every year in her honor—a graduation cap with her name on it and the date she would have received her high school diploma.

And then there had been the lectures from his family, the rules and consequences, the ones he'd balked at and fought.

The ones his parents had instigated because they loved him so much.

He'd do the same for little Jack.

Hell, he knew he'd make mistakes. But he'd do his

damnedest to raise his son to be the kind of man his own father would be proud of.

They passed ranches and farmland, the open terrain, steep cliffs, ridges and deep canyons that made the majestic La Plata Mountains, the Sleeping Ute Mountain and the sharp-hewn silhouette of Mesa Verde a home for locals and a tourist draw for travelers far and wide.

Jack babbled noisily and Aspen turned to talk to him. "When you get bigger I'll take you to the Ute Mountain Rodeo," she said, and Dylan bit his tongue to keep from correcting her—*We'll take you to the Ute Mountain Rodeo.*

"And we'll visit the Cortez Cultural Arts Center so you can see the Indian dances and artwork of our people," she continued. "The Bear Dance is in June. Legend says it all began when a man went to sleep and had a dream about a bear. In the dream, he thought if he went up into the mountains, the bear would teach him something of great strength. And so he did."

She paused and Jack made a cooing sound as if he enjoyed the sound of her voice and understood the meaning of the story.

"The bear gave him words of wisdom and taught him the bear dance, so he came down and shared it with his people," she continued. "When you get bigger, we'll go to the Mesa Verde National Park to see the celebration. They have a big balloon ride every year and you can watch the colorful balloons float across the sky. Most of the time our Ute people dress in regular clothes, in jeans and dresses, but a long time ago the women wore deerskin dresses and the men wore beachcloths. You'll see some of that at the festivals and dances."

By the time they arrived at the small house in the heart of Cortez, Dylan had learned more about the Ute history from Aspen than he'd ever learned in school. He'd developed a newfound respect for the plight of her people and her devotion to passing on the customs and stories of her ancestors.

The archaeology of the Mesa Verde cities was renowned and had inspired artists for years, the house where they were going to be staying was an adobe cottage that sat on top of a ridge and fit into the sweeping cliffs as if it had been carved naturally from the land.

Except this house had been fitted with a high-tech security system and a view of the mountainside to provide privacy and security for those who needed refuge from the world.

"It's beautiful," Aspen said as she carried Jack inside, and Dylan retrieved their luggage.

"I'm glad you like it." The space suddenly felt very intimate with the three of them inside. She offered him a tentative smile, and Jack cooed up at him from her arms. For a moment, Dylan savored the brief reprieve from the reality they'd left behind and imagined that this was their home.

That he and Aspen and Jack were a real family. That tonight they would put their son to bed.

Then they would fall into their own sanctuary together and make love until dawn.

And for once in his life, there wasn't a hit man or a serial killer lurking to destroy their happiness.

ASPEN'S SKIN PRICKLED with awareness as Dylan watched her settle Jack into the infant seat in the

Mexican tiled kitchen. She'd felt close to him in the car, admired the way he talked about his family and the affectionate tone to his words. He obviously loved them deeply.

What would it be like to be loved like that? To have a family unit who shared hopes and dreams yet still managed to maintain a close bond in the face of turbulent times?

Sadness welled in her chest. She missed her mother and Emma, and wanted her son to have the kind of family Dylan had described.

A family with a mother and a father.

But she had to be careful who she let into their lives.

Jack waved his fist at her and whimpered. He was probably hungry, so she stirred rice cereal into a bowl with the formula she'd heated from his bottle, making it soupy enough for him to swallow. Then she settled down in a chair to feed him.

He gulped down a few bites, spitting out half of it. She laughed. "I know it's not so tasty," she said, "but at least it's not grasshoppers." She scooped up another bite full and pressed the tip of the spoon to his lips, smiling as he sucked in the liquid mush.

"Tourists always ask what we Indians like to eat," she said softly. "Of course, we like modern food and fruits and vegetables. But they want to know about our past." She made a soaring noise with her mouth, swooping toward him with another spoonful as if they were playing a game. He followed the movement with his eyes, opening his mouth wide to slurp the cereal. "Years ago, it's true, that the Utes liked to eat grasshoppers and other insects. The Spanish thought it was disgusting, but they ate eggs and we thought that was gross, too."

Dylan moved up behind her and laughed as Jack puffed up his lips and blew bubbles, making cereal dribble down his chin.

"You'll like fish and meat better, little *mijo,*" Dylan said in a low voice. "Just wait and I'll teach you how to fish."

Aspen froze, her heart sputtering as she turned to look into his eyes. Why would he make a promise like that to her son when they both knew as soon as he caught Perkins and Watts, he'd be out of their lives?

DYLAN REALIZED WHAT HE'D SAID and had to back away. He'd allowed his love for his son and his dreams of fatherhood to destroy his concentration and had almost blurted out the truth to Aspen.

The fact that she didn't remember him or that he'd fathered her baby sent a white-hot rage through him. But the fact that she hadn't told him about their baby drove the pain deeper inside.

Jerking himself away from the table, he turned to retrieve the files they'd confiscated from the prison warden.

"Dylan?" Aspen asked softly.

"Just take care of the baby. I have work to do."

Her look of hurt and confusion added to his guilt, but his own emotions were too raw now for him to even try to explain. The Feds and local police were watching out for Perkins and Watts.

Better bury himself in the job and find out if Turnbull was alive, or if a copycat had surfaced.

He spread the files on the desk in the den, searching

through Turnbull's visitor log. In the past year, he'd had a couple of visitors—a woman named Sally Ann McCobb, and his half brother, Freddy.

Freddy had been present in court. The man had looked so different from the shaggy-headed, tattooed, burly Turnbull that Dylan would never have put them in the same family. But during the trial, he'd learned that Turnbull was half Ute. His mother had married a Ute man and lived on the reservation with him, while Freddy had been born of her first marriage to a man in Utah.

He jotted down both names to follow up on, noting the dates of their visits. Sally Ann McCobb had visited two weeks before Turnbull had been transferred, the half brother only three days.

He'd check them both out.

Next, he scanned the phone calls and found both Sally Ann and Freddy on the list, along with two other women.

There were stacks of letters from other fans to sort through, so he put those aside to look over after Aspen and Jack went to bed.

Then he checked the list of inmates and friends Turnbull had acquired in prison. One name on the list made his blood turn to ice.

Larry Gerome Sawyer—aka the Slaughterer.

He had killed over twelve women in a bloodbath that had rocked the Northern Ute tribe.

Dylan had also worked that case. Like Turnbull, the con hated his guts.

His heart raced as he checked the list of prisoners being transported with Turnbull.

The pendulum of questions began to swing back and forth in his head. Dear God.

Had Turnbull and Sawyer been partners of sorts? Had one or both of them planned the escape and walked away alive?

HE PRIDED HIMSELF on watching the news. He kept up with politics, with the economy, the stock market, but mostly he had a fetish for the crime.

A chuckle rumbled from him as he watched the news anchor.

"Aspen Meadows, the Ute woman who was missing for several weeks, has been found and is safe and alive. Preliminary reports stated that she was suffering from amnesia, but recently her memory has returned. She admitted that she witnessed two men dumping federal agent Julie Grainger's body along the river. The men have been identified as Boyd Perkins, a man believed to be a hit man for a local mob family, and Sherman Watts, a local Ute man who has assisted Perkins in evading the law."

He pressed his hand to his chest and laughed. The damn Feds thought they were setting a trap, but he was smarter than them.

And he'd been lying low. He'd had time to plan.

Their scheme would backfire in their faces.

He looked down at the blood on the girl's neck and imagined Acevedo's face when he found her, her neck slashed, her eyes panicked in terror, her mouth wide-open in a scream.

He had to find a public place to dump her body, some place significant, some place that would mean something to Acevedo.

Some place he couldn't resist leaving Aspen to come to.

He knew the place.

Yes, Acevedo would find her and see her blood in his dreams for the rest of his life.

Then he'd feel vulnerable, guilty, unworthy, imprisoned by the people he couldn't save, as well as the ones he'd put behind bars.

So sweet that he would think the Ute Slicer was back.

Of course he wouldn't know his identity. Wouldn't know if it was Turnbull's knife that had killed the girl or someone who just admired his handiwork.

Not until it was too late and Aspen Meadows was dead.

Chapter Fourteen

Aspen found the kitchen pantry and refrigerator stocked, as well as the nursery. After feeding Jack, she filled the baby bathtub full of warm water, stripped Jack and placed him inside with the rubber duck toy. He chased the little yellow duck as it floated around him as she bathed him, then scrunched up his nose in distaste when she soaped his hair with baby shampoo, then rinsed out the soap. But he seemed infatuated with the bubbles in the water and slapped at them with his hand.

"I'm glad you're taking this so well," she said. "You don't even seem to mind moving around."

While she didn't adjust quite so easily to change. She'd grown up on the reservation and, except for her college days, had never considered living anywhere else. Maybe that was the reason she hadn't kept Jack's father in the picture.

Or maybe he hadn't cared for Jack or her at all.

The water was growing cold, so she wrapped Jack in a bath towel, carried him to the dresser/changing table and laid him down. He kicked and swatted at the towel as she dried him off, then powdered his bottom and diapered him.

"You smell so sweet," she said as she wrestled with a little blue sleeper she found in the drawer. She snuggled him to her, then sat down in the rocking chair and read him a picture book, pointing out the simple objects on the colorful pages and smiling as he tried to grab the book and stuff the corners in his mouth.

A few minutes later, he dozed to sleep, and she rose and tucked him into the crib, covering him with a blanket. "Good night, little one. Sleep good." She kissed her hand, then pressed it to his cheek. "One day we won't be running," she whispered. "One day we'll be home to stay. And you can play with the other children on the reservation and learn to fish on the land. And we'll never have to leave home again."

When she turned to leave the room, Dylan stood at the door watching her, his gaze so intense that she froze. "What?" she whispered.

"You will be safe," he said quietly. "I promise you, Aspen. One day you and Jack won't have to look over your shoulders anymore."

The fact that he claimed they'd made love for a week taunted her. The kiss they'd shared proved the heat was still there, too, the embers of the fire simmering, waiting to be stoked.

She wondered if he was thinking about that week. If he ever regretted them parting.

And if being here alone with her and Jack might tempt him to come back to her bed.

Suddenly his look turned shuttered, as if he'd read her thoughts and had already answered them. And the answer was no.

Then he turned and left the room. She wanted to go

after him. To see if they could rekindle whatever they'd had. But she couldn't.

She had to think of Jack and their future.

She didn't want to be left with a broken heart, or for her son to cry after a man who didn't want him.

DYLAN LEFT THE ROOM before he gave into temptation and kissed Aspen.

And admitted that he was Jack's father.

He wanted her to remember, dammit, and explain why she'd left him out of their lives. Why she'd indicated to Lightfoot that she hadn't considered him father material, and that she hadn't felt anything more for him than lust.

While he'd thought about her every day while he was away.

Damn. He had to focus. He had a stack of letters to Turnbull to check out. It was hard to believe that instead of being terrified of serial killers as one would expect, that some killers drew fans—groupies. That some women actually felt sorry for the bastards and thought their love could save the men's sorry souls.

Foolish, sick, dysfunctional—and a growing problem that still baffled him to no end.

He reviewed the names he'd collected so far. Sally Ann McCobb, the female who'd visited Turnbull in jail. Freddy, the half brother.

And Larry Gerome Sawyer—the Slaughterer.

He had to know if Sawyer had died in the crash.

Wiping his clammy hands on his jeans, he punched the number for the state ME. The man answered on the third ring.

"Hi, Doc, this is Dylan Acevedo with the Bureau."

"Yeah, I've been talking with your brother. I already told him I'd let you guys know when I finished the results."

Impatience gnawed at Dylan. "That means you haven't confirmed that Turnbull is dead yet?"

"The partial dental plate suggests it was him, but I'm conducting more tests to verify since the plate wasn't in the man's mouth."

"How about the other bodies?" Dylan asked. "Who have you identified?"

"For sure, the bus driver, the guards and one of the prisoners."

"Which one?"

"A guy named Barry Burgess—inmates called him Buffalo. Man wore a size seventeen shoe, so his remains were the most obvious. And dental records confirmed the rest."

"How about Larry Gerome Sawyer?"

"I'm working on his body and the one we think is Turnbull's now."

Frustration knotted Dylan's shoulders. "You heard that a woman was killed using Turnbull's MO. We need to act quickly. Let me know as soon as you get the results."

The ME gave a long, labored sigh. "Listen, I haven't slept in over twenty-four hours. I'm working as fast as I can."

Dylan hung up and rubbed the back of his neck, trying to massage away the knots. It was too late to visit Sally Ann McCobb tonight or go to the prison, but he would do both in the morning.

Still, he could do some background work tonight.

He tapped into the federal databases and plugged in

the woman's name. A few minutes later, he had the scoop on Sally Ann.

She was in her thirties, had worked as a hairdresser for years, and recently gone back to school to study psychology. She'd first contacted Turnbull under the guise of research for a paper she was writing.

His interest piqued, he dug deeper. She had no record, no arrests, not even a parking ticket. Although she had been in counseling before she enrolled in the community college.

Counseling for spousal abuse.

The pieces fit with the general profile of prisoner groupies. He copied down her address, anxious to question the woman.

With Larry Gerome Sawyer on his mind, he accessed the files on his trial and crimes. The gruesome, bloody photos of a half-dozen women spilled onto the screen.

His stomach churned as he noted the details of his vicious attacks, stirring memories of the case. Memories he'd tried to banish.

Behind him, Aspen gasped. He stiffened, then turned to see her looking over his shoulder, her wide terrorized eyes glued to the photographs.

Dear God, he hadn't meant for her to see them or to know that another sick man just like Turnbull might be coming after her.

ASPEN STARED AT THE PICTURES of the bloody, naked bodies in front of her in horror.

She'd known Dylan was working but she'd assumed it had something to do with her and the trap they'd set for Perkins and Watts.

Yet he'd told her about the case he'd investigated before they'd met. Violent crime work was his job. Not just his job but his life.

"What are you doing?" she whispered.

He immediately shut down the file and stood. "I'm sorry. I didn't mean for you to see those."

She tried to recover, but she couldn't shake the images from her mind. "How do you do it?"

"Do what?"

"Investigate those crimes. Look at those dead women and not fall apart."

He reached out and stroked her arms. "I do sometimes," he said softly. Gently he lifted his hand and pushed her hair from her cheek. "The night we met. I was on the edge that evening. When I caught up with Turnbull, I wanted to kill him. Not lock him up but make him suffer the way he made those young women suffer." His tone dropped a decibel. "But then I met you and you brought me back to the brink of sanity."

Aspen's heart began to race. His touch felt so tender, but she heard the torment in his voice. "We talked about the case," she whispered.

He nodded. "I talked. You listened. You even thanked me for what I did." He gave a self-deprecating laugh. "I wasn't a hero that night, Aspen. I almost killed Turnbull in cold blood. Almost turned into a monster like him."

Aspen smiled, then reached up and pressed her hand to his cheek. "You could never be like him. He viciously destroyed innocent people's lives. Not just the women's lives he killed but their families and loved ones. You are a hero—you sought justice for them when they couldn't speak for themselves."

He shook his head as if he still didn't believe her, and Aspen's lungs tightened. No wonder she had slept with him the first night she'd met him. He was the sexiest, most honorable man she'd ever met. After working grueling hours to catch a killer and protect lives, he'd needed someone to comfort him.

So he'd turned to her.

How could she have resisted?

How could she resist him now?

She couldn't. She slid her hand into his hair and pulled him toward her, then stood on her tiptoes and pressed her lips to his. He growled low in his throat and yanked her to him as if he'd been waiting on an invitation.

He tasted like coffee and strength and man, a tantalizing flavor that made her crave more. He probed her lips apart with his tongue, then slipped inside to tease her as he deepened the kiss. She moved against him, her body bursting into an erotic song and dance that begged to partner with him.

He slid his arms over her shoulders and back, massaging her as he pulled her into him. His erection pulsed against her abdomen, sending a torrent of sensations through her. His hand found her breast, stroking, teasing, making desire surge through her.

No wonder she had stayed in bed for a week with this man.

She wanted to drag him there now and make love to him all night. To feel the pleasure his fingers and mouth evoked, to sate the burning need deep inside her.

He kneed her legs apart, pressing his hard length into the juncture between her thighs, and she grew moist with want. With a low groan, he dragged his mouth from hers and dipped his head to drop tongue lashes along her neck and throat, then downward until she arched her head backward and purred her delight.

A second later, his fingers traced her nipple through her blouse, and she groaned his name, hoping he'd follow the erotic touch with his mouth.

He didn't disappoint.

He slowly unbuttoned her blouse, parting the sheer fabric until he exposed the lace covering her breasts. His soft murmur of appreciation fueled her passionate response, and she reached for his shirt, anxious to feel bare chest against bare chest.

But he halted her movements by shoving her hands away, tugging her bra down and lowering his mouth to her nipple. He flicked his tongue over the pebbled bud, sending a spasm of need from her chest to her abdomen, then he closed his lips around the turgid peak, and she moaned. He wrapped his arms around her as her legs buckled, and he pulled the tip between his teeth, nipping, then suckling her until she thought she'd die from the pure pleasure of his wet tongue.

"Dylan, let's go to bed," she whispered, clutching him so her legs didn't give way.

Ignoring her, he moved his mouth to her other breast, loving it the same way, and heat shot through her, the yearning so intense that she slid her hand down to cup his sex. He was hard and full and ready.

She wanted him inside her, loving her, reminding her of the week they'd spent together, making her feel alive.

A sound jarred her from her euphoria. Jack. He was crying.

Dylan stiffened, slowly flicking his tongue over her

one more time, then letting go to search her face. His eyes were glazed, his breathing erratic, the stark need in his eyes mirroring the frantic pounding of her heart.

But Jack whimpered again, and she gave him a look of regret. "I guess I'd better check on him."

He gave a clipped nod, and she left the room. Although when she glanced over her shoulder, he was still watching her, his eyes smoldering, and a warm tingling spread through her. Maybe later they could take up where they'd left off.

But as soon as she saw Jack, reality intervened. What in the world was she thinking? She couldn't get involved with Dylan, not when he would leave them both.

Not when she didn't even remember the past and the name of Jack's father.

Or whether he might resurface again and want to be a part of their lives.

HIS INSTINCTS warned Dylan it was better that Jack had awakened and stopped him from making love to Aspen. But his body betrayed all rational logic and throbbed in protest.

He wanted Aspen just as much as he'd wanted her the very first time he'd seen her.

No. He wanted her more.

He walked to the nursery door and saw her lifting Jack into her arms, and his heart swelled with longing. These two people could be his family.

Jack already was, although Aspen seemed to have no idea.

And until she did and explained why she hadn't told him he had a son, he couldn't take her to his bed.

His cell phone trilled, jarring him from the moment, and he forced himself to back away and answer it. "Acevedo speaking."

"Dylan, it's Martinez. You're not going to like this, but we found another body. A Ute woman, early twenties."

Dylan bowed his head. "Same MO as the Ute Slicer?"

"I'm afraid so."

Dylan cursed and glanced at the nursery door where Aspen stood holding Jack. His heart slammed into his ribs.

If this killer came after her, he'd have to go through him first.

Chapter Fifteen

By the time Aspen rocked Jack back to sleep and returned to the living room, Dylan looked sullen. He was sorting through a stack of letters on the table and didn't even glance up when she stepped up beside him and placed her hand on his shoulder.

She wanted to pick up where they'd left off, but sensed he had withdrawn.

"Dylan?"

He stilled, dropped the envelope on the table and drew in a deep breath. "Go to bed, Aspen."

She felt the tension in his shoulder and rubbed the knot. "Why don't you come, too?"

His breath gushed out, but he didn't move to get up. Instead, he pulled away from her touch. "I have work to do."

Anger and confusion suffused her. "What kind of game are you playing?"

He finally turned and her breath caught at the intense expression in his eyes. Hunger was there, burning raw and bright, but also something akin to fear.

And maybe anger.

Déjà vu struck her. It was the same kind of dangerous look he'd had when she'd first met him. As if he was barely holding on to his ironclad control. As if he wanted to assuage the pain of the victims' faces that haunted him. As if he didn't deserve that reprieve.

"Please, Dylan," she said softly. "You've been working day and night."

His jaw tightened, and he finally stood and faced her, placing his hands on both of her arms. "And I'll keep working until I know that you're completely safe."

"We are safe here tonight," she said, hating to plead, but they both needed comfort.

"Maybe," he said in a deep voice. "But we just set the trap today. I have to stay focused and alert."

Disappointment made Aspen back away. She couldn't remember, but she didn't think she'd ever asked a man—begged a man—to go to bed with her.

She wouldn't do it again.

"Try to get some rest," she said, then she turned and fled to the bedroom before she forgot her promise to her son and convinced Dylan to make love to her anyway.

REFUSING ASPEN'S INVITATION was one of the most difficult things Dylan had ever done. His body hummed with arousal, literally ached from wanting to join her in bed, but the phone call earlier had reminded him that Aspen was in more danger than even she thought.

That a madman, as well as Perkins and Watts, might be after her.

And all because of him.

He spent the next few hours going over the letters

from the women who'd written Turnbull. The man had received hate mail along with letters from holy rollers who claimed they'd pray for his soul, and two other women who had offered conjugal visits. One from a lady in Nevada, another from a woman in New Jersey.

By 5:00 a.m., he called Ryan and asked him to contact someone in those states and check out the two women in case they'd recently been contacted by Turnbull or had helped him escape. He also asked Ryan to come and watch Aspen so he could follow up on the prisoners and Sally Ann McCobb.

Ryan was at the house by six. "I could go to the prison and talk to this woman," Ryan suggested.

Dylan shook his head. "No, I want to do it myself. Turnbull pledged revenge against me." Besides, he needed to put some physical space between him and Aspen.

Jack and Aspen were both still sleeping, so he left and drove to the prison first.

Warden Fernandez didn't appear surprised to see him. "I figured you'd show up sooner or later."

Dylan shook his hand and claimed the wooden chair across from the warden's desk. "I spoke with the state ME last night. It looks like both of your guards received wounds that suggest an attempted prison break. He's identified Burgess's body but is still working on Turnbull's and Sawyer's."

"Two of our most notorious," Fernandez muttered. "Frankly, I was glad they were being transferred. Both were cold-blooded psychopaths."

"Did either of them have any friends in here?"

"Friends?" Fernandez gave a sarcastic grunt. "I'm not sure either man knew what a friend was. Turnbull stabbed Sawyer and was in solitary the last few days before he was transferred."

"So they teamed up? That doesn't make sense."

He shrugged. "They were both tough bastards. Neither one showed any remorse."

And if the two of them had escaped and paired up—God help them all.

"Can I speak to Turnbull's former cell mate?"

"Sure." He punched a button on his intercom and ordered one of the guards to bring the man to a holding room, then gestured for Dylan to follow.

They passed through security, and Dylan stood by the wooden table in the interrogation room while the guard escorted Carl Tanner, a short, bald, robust guy in handcuffs and leg irons into the room.

Tanner was a doctor who'd killed his wife because she'd had an affair. Compared to Turnbull and Sawyer, he was a damn saint.

Although the snarl on his pocked face didn't look saintly.

Dylan produced his badge and introduced himself.

Tanner angled his head to the left. "What do you want?"

"I need to talk to you about Frank Turnbull."

A grin curled the man's lips. "Heard that son of a bitch died."

"That's what I want to discuss. There's a possibility he might not have been killed in the crash. That he could have escaped. Or that a copycat is imitating his crimes." He explained about the two murders following Turnbull's MO.

Tanner whistled. "So. What's it got to do with me?"

"You were his cell mate for a while. Were you two buddies?"

"Hell, no. Turnbull didn't make friends." Tanner yanked open the top buttons of his shirt, revealing a set of deep scars. "He did that with a fork. So, he definitely ain't no friend of mine."

That would work to his favor. "Did he talk to you about escaping?"

Tanner chuckled. "All the damn time. That and getting revenge on the man who put him in here."

"Did he ever mention a partner? Admit that he worked with someone to commit the Ute Slicer murders?"

Tanner shook his head. "Man like him wants control. He wouldn't have a damn partner—he likes to work alone so he can bask in all the glory."

Dylan's frustration mounted. He needed something new, concrete. "How about a name or a contact? Someone who would have helped him try to escape?"

Tanner leaned forward with his beefy arms on the table. "What you gonna do for me if I tell you?"

"What do you want?"

Pain flashed in Tanner's eyes. "To see my kid. I haven't seen him since I've been in. I want to tell him how sorry I am."

Dylan twisted his mouth in thought. "I'll see what I can do."

Tanner worked his mouth side to side. "Some bleached-blond bimbo used to visit him. Name was Sally Ann. He told me he hated the bitch but she'd do anything for him."

Tanner shook his head. "I don't get it. I get hate mail for killing my cheating wife, and he murders girls for fun and women write him love letters."

"You're right, it doesn't make sense," Dylan agreed.

"But a lot of crimes don't." He hesitated. "Can you think of anyone else?"

Tanner shrugged. "His half brother, Freddy. Seems he felt indebted to Turnbull for something but he never said why."

Dylan thanked him and stood. Maybe Freddy had paid off his debt by helping Turnbull escape.

ASPEN STUMBLED INTO THE kitchen to make coffee and was surprised to find Agent Tom Ryan sitting at the table instead of Dylan.

She frowned, grateful she'd thrown on a pair of jeans and sweater instead of wearing her pajamas. "Where's Dylan?"

Tom glanced up from his notes. "He wanted to pursue some leads, so you're stuck with me for a few hours."

She poured herself a cup of coffee and went to look out the window. Situated at the top of the ridge, she had a sweeping view of the land, the snow-capped mountaintops, the shrubs and grass in the canyon that would be turning green as soon as spring resurrected life back to the parched land.

Why had Dylan gone instead of letting one of the other agents pursue the leads?

Because he wanted to get away from you.

She sipped the hot coffee, renewing her vow not to push him again. Obviously whatever they'd shared when they'd first met had meant nothing to him. She was just a case now that he had to finish. A witness to protect.

Not the woman he loved.

"You shouldn't stand in front of the window," Agent Ryan said. "It's too dangerous."

A chill rippled through her at his warning, and she backed away, suddenly angry and claustrophobic. "I hate this," she muttered. "Hate being afraid. Hiding out. Wondering if or when someone might come out of nowhere and strike."

"We have agents watching your house. We'll get them."

She whirled around. "But it's so unfair. He has the control, the power."

"It'll be over soon, Aspen. You just have to hang in there and trust Dylan."

Trust Dylan? That was the ironic thing. She *had* trusted him from the moment he'd picked her up at the shelter.

Jack whimpered from the nursery, and she forced her thoughts about Dylan to the back of her mind. Her baby needed her.

And she would do whatever she had to do to protect him and give him a good life.

Her mother had raised her alone and managed. Somehow, she would do the same.

If only she could stop wishing Dylan would be a part of her life.

DYLAN DROVE TO EAGLE'S LANDING to see Freddy, but the man wasn't home. He found a work address from the database and headed to the garage where Freddy was supposed to work.

A skinny man, probably midforties, wearing grease-stained coveralls and smoking a cigarette loped toward him. "What you want, mister?" He gestured toward Dylan's car. "Need some work done?"

"No." Dylan removed his ID from his pocket and

flashed it. "Name is Special Agent Acevedo. I need to speak to one of your employees, Freddy Lakers."

The man took a drag of his cigarette and blew smoke through his nose. "Freddy ain't showed up at work for going on a week now."

Dylan frowned. "Has he called in? Anyone here heard from him?"

"Nope, not a word." The man puffed on his cigarette again. "But if he does show up, I'm gonna fire his ass."

Dylan gave him his card, told him if he heard from him to call him, then climbed back in his car. He checked Sally Ann's address and turned onto the street, then headed toward Crescent Canyon.

On the drive, his mind raced back to the night before, to the fact that Aspen had wanted him.

And not because she remembered their time in Vegas together.

A smile curved his mouth as a thought struck him. Maybe their time in Vegas hadn't just been a heat-of-the-moment affair. The fact that she wanted him again now meant there might be something deeper between them.

But how could they have a relationship with secrets and lies still between them?

HE KNEW WHERE ASPEN MEADOWS WAS hiding.

He'd followed Acevedo and watched him escort the Ute woman inside that house on the mountain. He thought she was safe.

But none of the Ute women were safe.

Only Aspen could wait a few hours.

First he had to pay a visit to another woman. One he'd fantasized about reuniting with for the past year.

One he wanted to kill.

But first he'd make her suffer.

He stared at the battered old house with hate churning in his gut. Here, his first evil thoughts had been born. Here, he'd fantasized about murder.

Ducking low, he wove between the shrubs and bushes surrounding her small wooden house, memories of her cruel beatings and preaching returning.

The paint on the house had faded and chipped over the years, the windowpanes were dirty, the porch sagging and rotting. He'd heard that his stepfather had long ago run out on her.

Not that he blamed him. The damn bitch would kill any love anyone had for her.

The house was dark inside, the lights off, and a mangy dog lay sprawled in front of the porch steps. He stopped to scratch behind his ears, then the wood floor squeaked as he climbed the rickety steps and let himself inside the house.

He paused to listen. A low humming sound echoed from the back room. He didn't bother to hide himself or keep his footfalls quiet. He wanted to see the look on her face when she saw him.

A minute later, her humming stopped. She'd heard his footsteps. He stood in the den by the ratty plaid sofa and remembered being forced to his knees while she ordered him to pray after one of her famous beatings.

He smelled her before she entered. The lemony scent of floor cleaner and dusting spray that still had the power to nauseate him. Then her rail-thin wrinkled face appeared in the doorway. She'd aged drastically, but those sharp eyes were just as mean.

"My lord," she gasped.

He grinned and reached for the knife at his belt. "Hello, Mama."

Chapter Sixteen

Sally Ann McCobb lived in an apartment outside Crescent Canyon. Dylan noted the weathered siding, the overgrown unkempt bushes and the broken-down car in the parking lot, frowning at the sight of a scruffy little boy riding a battered tricycle on the sidewalk.

Sally Ann lived on the bottom floor, so he knocked on the door. He'd considered calling first, but wanted the element of surprise on his side.

He paced while he waited, and when no one answered knocked again, and finally heard footsteps shuffling toward the door. A minute later, a bleached blonde with red puffy eyes, a swollen lip and a bruise on her left cheek squeaked the door open.

Dylan flashed his ID. "Special Agent Dylan Acevedo."

Her eyes widened perceptively for a brief moment of panic before a resigned look settled over her features. "Yeah?"

"You're Sally Ann McCobb?"

She gave a slight nod. "I ain't done nothing wrong."

Dylan offered her a smile. "No one said you have. I just need to talk to you, that's all, ma'am." The wind whipped through him, swirling dust and a fast-food wrapper around his feet. "Can I come in?"

She hesitated, then seemed to decide she had no choice, and unfastened the chain and allowed him entry. The inside of her place was no more impressive than the outside, with cheap, worn furniture and a battered oak table in the kitchen/den combination.

He immediately scanned the room, searching for a sign that a man had been there. One coffee cup on the table, not two. Although an empty bottle of whiskey lay atop the overflowing trash.

Turnbull liked whiskey.

Sally Ann tugged a faded chenille housecoat around her plump shoulders. She didn't look like Turnbull's type.

"I think you know the reason I'm here," he said.

She twisted her mouth sideways, biting on her lip, then went to the coffeepot and poured herself another cup. "You want some?" she asked.

He nodded, not really wanting it but deciding to stay in her good graces as long as he could. She didn't ask if he wanted sugar or creamer, just handed him the chipped mug and he took a swig, nearly choking on the potent brew.

"You've been writing Frank Turnbull in prison?"

The nervous flicker of her eyes gave her away. "I was doing research for a class I'm taking." She tapped a pack of cigarettes against her palm, pulled one out and lit it. "I talked to several prisoners."

"But you continued writing Turnbull, didn't you? Personal letters? *Love* letters?"

She blew out a plume of smoke. "I guess you already

know that. So why don't you cut to the chase. You're wondering why a woman would write love letters to a prisoner."

He gave a clipped nod. "You know how many women he killed?"

"Yes. But that was before he found Jesus."

And she'd bought that dog and pony show? "Do you know where he is now?"

"Heard he died in a bus crash being transferred to ADX."

His gaze met hers, that flicker of unease giving her away again. "That's what he wants people to believe, isn't it?"

She took another drag on her cigarette, then thumped the ashes into a foam cup on the counter. "That's what happened."

He made a low sound in his throat, deciding to change tactics. "So, Sally Ann, how did you get those bruises?"

"My ex beat me," she said matter-of-factly.

"I thought you were finished with him."

"I am."

"How about Turnbull? If he survived, would you help him?"

"If he survived that crash?" She gave a sarcastic cackle. "Hell, yeah. If I didn't, he'd kill me."

"But you're not his type," Dylan said.

"I know," she said in a pained voice. "That's what he told me. He likes Ute girls."

"Not for sex," Dylan said.

She shook her head. "Not for anything."

He walked over and picked up the bottle of whiskey. "You drink all this yourself, Sally Ann?"

A panicked look shot through her eyes. That look alone was enough to send a cold chill through Dylan. "He was here, wasn't he? And he gave you those bruises?"

Pain darkened her expression. "I loved him," she whispered hoarsely. "I really thought he'd changed. That he'd found the Lord and we could have a life."

Dylan gritted his teeth. "Did he say where he was going?'

"I told you he's dead." Sally Ann gestured toward the door. "But he had a groupie, some guy who wrote him and thought he was a god. Turnbull told me about him during my last visit."

"Did he give you a name?"

"He called himself Ulysses. Said he was going to make Frank's work look like child's play. And that he'd start the game all over again."

Dylan's mind raced. Was Turnbull alive? Or had this man taken on his MO?

"Did Turnbull mention having dental work done lately?"

She stubbed out her cigarette with an annoyed grunt. "Yeah, so?"

"So far, the only concrete evidence that Turnbull might have died in the crash was a partial bridge."

Her face paled.

Dylan's patience snapped. "What? You have to tell me if you know something. We can protect you."

A tense heartbeat passed between them before she replied. "I think that guy Ulysses was a dentist."

Dammit.

His stomach in a cold knot of dread, he grabbed the whiskey bottle with a handkerchief and carried it to his car to drop by the crime lab. If it had Turnbull's prints on it, they'd know for sure that he was alive.

He also had to track down this guy Ulysses. Find out where he lived.

If he was copycatting Turnbull or if they'd teamed up together.

And he had to do it before either one of them found Aspen.

A chill invaded him. If one or both of them had been watching Aspen and him, they knew she wasn't at her home. Could they have followed him to the safe house?

He'd taken every precaution. But still anxiety ripped through him, and as he drove toward the crime lab, he phoned Ryan to warn him to stay alert.

ASPEN HATED that Dylan had left her alone. Tom Ryan was a nice man, tried to be unobtrusive, but having a stranger guarding her drove home the fact that Dylan was only back in her life because of this case.

So did the news clip that aired on TV, a repeat of the earlier broadcast.

"Police have now confirmed that a missing Ute woman, Aspen Meadows, has been found safe and alive. Although preliminary reports stated that she was suffering from amnesia, Miss Meadows's memory has returned.

"The woman witnessed two men dumping the body of Special Agent Julie Grainger on the Ute reservation.

"Those men have been identified as Sherman Watts—" the reporter paused while they flashed Watts's picture on the screen "—and Boyd Perkins—" another pause to show his photograph "—who is believed to be a hit man.

"Police have issued an APB for both men and a manhunt is underway.

"Meanwhile, Miss Meadows has agreed to testify against the men when they are apprehended. If you have any news about either Perkins or Watts and their whereabouts, please contact the FBI immediately."

Aspen shivered. There was no going back now. She only hoped that the two men took the bait and came after her at her house.

She spread a blanket on the floor and arranged several baby toys around Jack, turning the jack-in-the-box crank handle until the clown popped up. A laugh bubbled from her son's throat, and she pushed the doll down inside and cranked the handle all over again.

Agent Ryan's cell phone trilled, and he glanced at it, then connected the call. "Hey, Acevedo."

She tensed, her nerves on edge as she listened to the one-sided conversation. As soon as Ryan disconnected the call, she asked him what Dylan had said.

"He's following some leads on the Turnbull investigation, then stopping by the lab to check in. He should be back in a couple of hours."

Aspen wanted more details. But Ryan stepped outside with his phone, cutting off her question. She'd have to wait on Dylan. The Turnbull case had obviously gotten under his skin, the reason he'd personally left to do the legwork.

Would the Ute Slicer come after Dylan for revenge?

The idea of something terrible happening to him sent a shudder through her.

Jack grew fussy, and she picked him up and walked him around, talking to him to soothe him. But he was hungry so she fixed another bottle, cradled him in the rocking chair and fed him.

"He has to come back," she whispered as Jack fell asleep. "He just has to."

When Jack dozed off, she laid him in the crib and covered him with a blanket. The door squeaked open and she hurried to the living room, hoping Dylan was back. But Agent Ryan had stepped back inside.

"Is something wrong?" she asked.

"No, I was just checking the perimeter," he said. "And I phoned Agent Parrish to see if Perkins or Watts showed up at your house."

"Have they?"

"No," he said. "But they still might. They're probably waiting until dark."

She nodded, and glanced at the clock. That was hours away. Hours of waiting and pacing and not knowing. Hours of hoping and praying the two men got caught.

Hours of wondering if that psycho Turnbull would come after Dylan.

WORRY NEEDLED DYLAN as he parked at the crime lab and rushed inside. He met Callie at the door of her office and held up the whiskey bottle. "Can you print this and run it right away? I need to know if Turnbull's prints are on it."

Her brow furrowed. "Where did you get it?"

He explained about the prison mail and visitor log.

"Did she admit that he was alive?" Callie asked.

Dylan shook his head. "No, but I read between the lines. I think he paid her a visit and she realized that his talk of redemption was bull."

With gloved hands, Callie took the bottle to her workstation, dusted it for prints then ran them through AFIS.

Dylan watched as she pulled up Turnbull's prints and the computer program worked its magic.

Seconds later, his fears were confirmed.

Turnbull had been at Sally Ann McCobb's house.

Which meant Turnbull was alive.

"Damn," Callie muttered. "How did that SOB walk away from that burning bus?"

"With help," Dylan said cryptically.

"Sally Ann?"

"No. Well, hell, she may have given him some money, but she's not bright enough or devious enough to pull this off." He hesitated, his mind working. "I couldn't locate his half brother, Freddy. I'm going to get an APB issued for him immediately. And Sally Ann McCobb mentioned that Turnbull had a fan. Called himself Ulysses." He snapped his fingers. "I probably have mail from him in that stack at the safe house, the pile I haven't gotten to. I'll analyze when it I get back there. Maybe it will lead us to his real name and address. My guess is that that corpse in the fire either belonged to his half brother or his fan."

Callie nodded and Dylan called the state ME to relay his findings.

"I did ID Sawyer," the ME said. "But there's something odd about the last body. Signs on the corpse indicate that the man suffered from a brain tumor."

"It's not Turnbull," Dylan said, then explained his discovery. "But you need to find out who he is." He told him to get Freddy's dental and medical records and to check DNA. And he needed to find out what this man Ulysses's full name was, if it was, in fact, his real name.

As soon as he hung up, his cell phone trilled. Bree. "Acevedo, you have to get over here. There's another woman's body. And you won't believe who it belongs to."

"Who?"

"Turnbull's mother." Her breathing sounded erratic.

Dylan disconnected, jogged toward his car and drove at a dead race toward the address Bree gave him.

When he climbed out, sweat beaded on his skin and he hurried up to the house.

As soon as he ducked below the crime tape, he met Bree. She was as pale as a ghost.

"It's bad," she said.

The metallic scent of blood and human wastes assaulted him as he entered. Then he saw the blood everywhere. Splattered on the walls and floor, the elderly woman's body sprawled on the kitchen tiles in a river of red where she'd been gutted.

Chapter Seventeen

Sheriff Martinez took Bree by the elbow. "Go outside. Get some air. Agent Acevedo and I have this one covered."

Bree didn't argue. She hurried outside as if she desperately needed fresh air. Dylan remembered her pregnancy and understood Patrick's reaction.

If he'd known Aspen was pregnant, he would have been just as protective.

The crime techs arrived to process the scene, but Dylan studied it, seeing the dark rage Turnbull had had for his mother.

"Who do you think did this?" Patrick asked.

Dylan gave a bitter laugh. "Turnbull. He escaped the crash and he's out here."

Patrick muttered a curse. "Why the overkill?"

"His mother was the source of his rage." Dylan grimaced. "Unfortunately, the past year in the pen has probably fueled his anger. And judging from this bloodbath, the viciousness of his crimes will probably escalate."

"That's all we need," Patrick mumbled.

Dylan grimaced. "Yeah. And if he's going after the people he thinks hurt him, then he's on a personal vendetta."

Which put him at the top of the list.

But he knew Turnbull. He was cunning. He wouldn't just try to kill him.

Just as he had gotten inside Turnbull's head when he'd profiled and interrogated him, Turnbull had gotten into his head. He knew the case had gotten to Dylan.

He'd recognized the vengeance in his eyes when he'd nearly killed the killer.

Cold sweat dotted his body and his heart hammered in his chest.

He'd make him suffer by hurting another woman.

Aspen.

He didn't know how Turnbull had figured out that he cared about her, but he had.

And that was where he'd strike.

The piece of thunderwood he'd left on her doorstep had been a statement.

He had to go back to her now. Trust his fellow agents and the cops to do their jobs.

Nothing else mattered except keeping Aspen and their son safe.

THE SUN HAD FADED behind dark storm clouds, night setting in. Aspen fed Jack and played with him on the pallet until he finally conked out again. She watched him breathing for a few minutes, still unable to believe she'd given birth to such a beautiful and wonderful child.

Finally the sound of a car engine split the tense silence, relief welling inside her as she looked out the window and spotted Dylan climb from the car.

Agent Ryan met him outside, and Aspen ached to

join them, but Tom had given her strict orders not to go outside for fear someone was watching.

She felt like a prisoner.

How long would this confinement last? Would she have to look over her shoulder for the rest of her life? Live in constant fear that someone would try to kill her?

Tears threatened, along with a deep desperation, but she willed herself to be strong and not fall apart.

It seemed like an eternity before Agent Ryan left and Dylan finally came inside. As soon as she saw the solemn expression on his face, she knew something was terribly wrong.

"What happened?" she asked.

Although anger simmered below the surface of his guarded calm, his blue eyes glimmered with emotions she couldn't read. He clenched and unclenched his fists. "Nothing. No hits on your house yet."

He was lying. "There's something else, Dylan. What is it?"

He shrugged. "Is Jack all right?"

"Yes," she said. "Now stop avoiding me. I need to know what's going on."

"You just have to trust me," he said, then walked into the kitchen for a glass of water. But his brow was furrowed and damp, his body language perched for battle, his senses alert as he combed through the house checking windows and locks.

He reminded her of a big cat, like a panther, stalking the place as if in search of prey—or a predator.

"Do you think Perkins or Watts know we're here?" she asked, her heart starting to race.

"No," he said a little too fast.

"You do, don't you?" She grabbed his arm and forced him to look at her. "Did they follow you?"

"No, I told you not to worry. I'll protect you."

Instead of consoling her or pulling her into his arms, he seemed cold, distant.

Impersonal.

"Damn you, Dylan. I don't understand you. You're lying, something is terribly wrong. I'm not an idiot."

"I know that," he said in a clipped tone. "I'm just doing my job."

Hurt and bewilderment speared her along with bitterness. "So I'm just a job to you now?"

His gaze met hers, and for a brief second, something else flickered in his eyes. Hunger. Desire.

Fear.

"Tell me what's going on, Dylan. One minute you're hot and hold and kiss me like you want me, and the next you look at me like I'm a perfect stranger, just some woman you have to protect for your damn job."

He tried to pull away, but she clawed at his arm. "You say we spent a week together, a week in bed, and when you kissed me before and we almost made love, I felt something intense between us. A heat I've never felt before." Her breath feathered out, choppy with her frustration and desperate need. "But now you act as if you don't care about me at all. How can you be so cold?"

A muscle ticked in his jaw, and he reached up and covered her hands as if to pull them away, but his touch was so warm, and she needed it so badly, she whispered his name again.

"Don't you care, Dylan? Don't you care at all?"

Tension stretched between them, her question echoing in the silence.

"Dylan, please," she said, hating the pathetic desperation in her voice. "Please don't shut me out. I need you."

There, she'd said it. Bared her soul and shed her own protective barriers.

"It's not that I don't care," he finally said in a gruff voice.

"Then why pull away from me?"

His mouth tightened as if answering her cost him. "Because I care too damn much."

Her breath caught in her throat along with a painful surge of longing, prompting her to lift one hand to his cheek. God help her, but she wanted him.

"Aspen, don't," he murmured.

But that plea reverberated with suppressed desire. Desire that mirrored the hunger he had to see reflected in her eyes.

He might leave her when the case was over. But she needed him now.

And with death knocking at her door, the moment was all that mattered.

ON SOME SUBCONSCIOUS LEVEL, Dylan knew he was crossing the line, that he should remain alert and not allow his personal feelings to clutter an already complicated and dangerous situation, but he'd lost that game a year ago when he'd first met Aspen.

No, before, when he'd nearly killed Turnbull just because he wanted to see the man die.

Only Aspen had saved him back then. Aspen and her

understanding. Aspen and her sultry looks, her tenderness and passion.

She'd reminded him that the world consisted of something other than ugliness and cruelty, that it could also be beautiful and loving.

Needing that reminder now, to hold on to the fact that she was alive and in his arms instead of in Turnbull's or this copycat's unmerciful hands, he dragged her into his arms and claimed her mouth with his.

Her lips tasted like ripe berries and sunshine and sweetness, causing his chest to clench with a warmth that helped to chase the chill from his body.

The chill that had dogged him ever since he'd found that piece of thunderwood on her doorstep.

The chill that had grown to insurmountable heights at the sight of the man's latest brutalized victim.

His mother.

Don't think about the case. Think about how wonderful it is to finally hold Aspen again. To finally be able to touch her and stroke her bare flesh and meld your body with hers.

She moaned low in her throat, and he delved his tongue inside her mouth, hungry and taking everything she offered.

He deepened the kiss, one hand plunging into her hair while the other one skated over her back, down to her waist, then her hips. He tugged her up against his hard body, his sex jutting against the fly of his slacks and brushing her thigh.

She whispered his name in a low purr as he tore his mouth from her lips and trailed kisses along the long slender column of her neck. His mouth watered for more, his length throbbing to be closer to her. He kneed her legs apart, and fit himself into the cradle of her thighs, then groaned when she arched her hips into him.

Raw need tore through him, and he slid his hand down to cup her breast, kneading the plump mound through her blouse until she begged him to remove her top.

One flick and buttons went flying. He ripped off the garment, her throaty sounds of approval spurring him on. Then her skirt came off, fell to the floor in a puddle, and he paused to drink in the sight of her beauty. Full breasts encased in ivory lace rose and fell with her erratic breathing.

"Dylan?"

"I'm here, baby." Dark fantasies sprang to mind as she reached for his shirt and hastily unfastened the buttons. Her fingers fired his flesh, enflamed him to the point that he thought he might explode with need.

Desperation turned the next few seconds into a frenzy as they yanked at each other's clothes, throwing them onto the floor.

Naked, she was a glorious sight to behold.

Her body was slightly rounder now she'd given birth, a soft lushness to it that, if possible, made him crave her even more.

He thought he'd memorized each inch of her, but as he explored the fine contours of her breasts, her hips and thighs, he knew his memory had failed to imprint her exquisitely soft skin or the exact dark brown of her nipples into his brain.

His senses sprang to life, soaking in her sweet feminine fragrance, his skin erupting with white-hot sensations as she traced her fingers over his bare chest and arms then lower to his abdomen.

He sucked in a sharp breath when she feathered touches on the insides of his thighs, and images of her on her knees pleasuring him flashed behind his eyes.

She had done it before. Tasted and tortured with him her tongue and lips, and he wanted her touch now.

But he had to taste her first.

Starved for her sweetness, he picked her up and carried her to the bedroom, then spread her on the bed to feast.

She moaned and clawed at his arms as he kissed her breasts, then pulled one hard tip into his mouth and suckled her. She arched her hips as if in silent invitation, but he forced her to wait while he loved her.

Teasing her thighs apart with his hand, he toyed with the soft curls at her center, loving her other breast until she pleaded his name.

"Dylan, please, I need you inside me."

"Soon, baby, soon," he whispered against her belly as he pressed kisses down her stomach to the treasure below.

He licked her folds, spreading her legs and jutting his tongue out to taste her heat. She whimpered, and tried to stop him, but he forced her still and fit his mouth over her core, sucking the heart of her desire until her honeyed juices flowed into his mouth.

She bucked upward, clenching and twisting the sheets between her fingers as she cried out her release.

Need enflamed him, his body aching with the relentless force of a man who needed to pump inside a woman.

And not just any woman.

Aspen.

The woman who'd soothed him a year ago, the

woman who'd reminded him that beauty still thrived in this godforsaken world of killers.

A woman who'd stolen his heart and, he feared, his very soul.

ASPEN CLOSED HER EYES, savoring the brilliant splash of colors sweeping her into euphoria.

The moment Dylan had touched her bare flesh, her inhibitions had fled like rain evaporating on a hot pavement.

Had it always been this way between the two of them? This explosive?

He rose above her, bracing himself on his hands. "Open your eyes, and look at me, Aspen." He nuzzled her neck with his lips and teeth.

"I want you to see me when I'm inside you."

Aspen did as he said, the pure raw passion glazing his eyes, sending spasms of erotic excitement through her.

Slowly he teased her center with his full hard length, back and forth in an exquisite torture that sent her over the edge again. She dug her fingernails into his arms and clung to him as he thrust deeper inside her, stretching and filling her until the memory of him binding himself with her flashed back, sweeping her into the vortex of desire that had robbed her breath a year ago, a hot yearning that had burned through her each time he'd touched her.

The present blended with the past, their dance of lovemaking familiar and overwhelming her.

He lifted her hips with his hands and thrust deeper, angling her so their bodies met so intimately that another orgasm rippled through her.

He hammered harder, faster, his own groan of satisfaction whispering in her ear as his release came, swift and potent.

For a long moment, he held himself inside her, their bodies quivering together as the aftermath of their passion ebbed and flowed.

And as the sensations overrode her earlier fear, another memory surfaced.

The moment she'd realized she was pregnant.

And that her son belonged to Dylan.

The realization rocked her world, and she froze as he turned her over in his arms and held her.

Her breath rushed out as she tried to piece together what had happened between them. She and Dylan had made a baby during their short affair. A beautiful little boy that she'd loved from the moment of conception.

But she hadn't told him he had a son.

And he was going to hate her for it.

DYLAN CRUSHED ASPEN IN HIS embrace, his chest heaving. He had needed her tonight, needed her sweetness, her loving.

Yet he felt her shutting down.

Only this time he refused to let her.

He pulled back slightly to look into her eyes. Dark brown eyes glazed with passion, and a hazy look of arousal that made him want her again.

But she stiffened in his arms and he felt her putting some distance between them just as he had last year when he'd guarded his heart.

"Dylan?" she said softly.

His chest tightened. "Yes?"

"I remembered something else."

"Something about your attack?"

She shook her head, and suddenly the truth dawned on him. "You remembered us being together?"

She nodded, a wariness filling her eyes.

"And what else?" he asked gruffly.

She clamped her teeth over her bottom lip and bit down as if debating on whether to confide in him.

"What?" he asked, his impatience mounting.

She sat up, tugging the sheet up around her, and he gritted his teeth, hating to do anything to encroach on the closeness they'd just shared.

But he had to know the truth.

"Tell me what you remember, Aspen."

She exhaled as if to steady her nerves. "I remember us making love last year. The week we spent together." A faint blush crept up her cheeks. "It was…wonderful."

He nodded.

"But then we parted."

"Yes. I got called away on an assignment."

"And I finished school and went back to the reservation to teach."

"That's right."

She hesitated. "And a few weeks later, I discovered I was pregnant."

His throat tightened as he waited, tension stretching between them. He wanted to prod her, shake her. "Go on."

Her gaze met his, the heat still simmering between them. But lies and secrets stood like a wall they needed to climb.

"Aspen, what else did you remember?"

Tears filled her eyes. "That you're Jack's father."

Chapter Eighteen

Dylan's heart swelled with her words, an overwhelming protective urge slamming into him. He would protect her and Jack with his life.

Yet anger that she'd kept the truth from him made him grit his teeth. "I know. Why didn't you tell me you were pregnant?"

Shock widened her eyes. "What do you mean, you know?"

"For God's sake, Aspen. I put two and two together, and wondered, so I took a DNA sample."

Hurt strained her features. "Why didn't you tell me? Why go behind my back?"

Hell, she was turning the tables on him?

"Why didn't I tell you?" He wanted to shake her. "Why didn't you tell me? Why didn't you contact me when you first realized you were pregnant?"

She pressed her fingers to her temple, massaging her head as if struggling with the memories.

"I did," she whispered. "I tried to contact you a few times, but the Bureau said you couldn't be reached, that you were out of the country."

He closed his eyes on a hiss, and when he opened them, she was watching him. "You should have tried harder."

Tears glittered in her eyes. "Why? You left without telling me where you were going, without asking me to see you again." Pain laced her voice and any bravado she had wilted.

"So why not try when he was born? You could have left messages. If I'd known, I would have come."

She stood, grabbed her robe, put it on and knotted it tightly then walked to the window and looked out.

Anger and fear choked him. He wanted to know the truth, yet what if she said that she hadn't wanted him in their son's life? That he was too dangerous?

ASPEN TREMBLED, hating the anger in Dylan's voice. But how could she blame him? She'd deprived him of knowing his son.

And his question raised her own insecurities and resurrected other memories.

"Why, Aspen?" Dylan asked. "Why didn't you call me when he was born?"

"I didn't want to feel like I'd trapped you."

"It wouldn't have been like that," he said. "Besides, I had a right to know."

"I know that," she whispered. "But I was afraid," she admitted.

"Afraid of what?" He gripped her arms and spun her around, his eyes icy cold. "You were afraid of me? Afraid I would hurt Jack? That I wouldn't be a good father because I told you I almost killed Turnbull?"

The distress in his voice made her heart clench. Then her conversation with Kurt Lightfoot rolled back.

He'd said that she was afraid of Jack's father, but that wasn't true. "I was afraid that you might try to take Jack away from me."

"What?" Hurt tinged his voice.

"I was afraid you'd want custody. That you wouldn't want me to raise Jack on the reservation." Her voice cracked. "And Kurt said that with your government job that you had power and money. That you probably knew people and could convince a judge to give Jack to you."

A sense of betrayal stabbed at him like a knife.

"You listened to Lightfoot instead of coming to me?" he said, his voice thickening. "You told him about our baby and not me. What did you plan to do, marry him and let him raise my son as his own?"

The very thought fueled irrational jealousy.

He had to get out of there. Couldn't look at her and think about her keeping his son from him and allowing Jack to call another man his father.

"No," Aspen whispered.

But he couldn't listen to her now. Couldn't look at her.

Couldn't stay in the room, wearing his feelings on his shoulder and knowing that she'd even contemplated such an idea.

Furious, he yanked on a pair of jeans and stormed from the room. He heard her calling his name, and he shouted for her to leave him alone.

He didn't look back to see her reaction. Instead, he stalked outside, slammed the door, jogged down the porch steps and glanced into the trees shrouding the ridge.

He leaned against a tree and closed his eyes, his chest heaving.

He had to regain his composure.

But suddenly a twig snapped behind him, and he opened his eyes, automatically reaching for his gun.

Dammit, he'd left it inside.

Before he could move to retrieve it, something sharp and hard slammed into his skull, and he collapsed on the ground, the world going black.

ASPEN'S HEART ACHED. She hadn't meant to hurt Dylan but she obviously had.

But she had to be honest with him. She'd wanted him to know about Jack, but she also hadn't wanted to pressure him into marriage or taking responsibility for their son.

She'd wanted him to come to her because he cared for her and wanted to be a part of her life.

Her own mother had faced the same dilemma and had opened herself up to Aspen's father, but he'd walked away without looking back. He'd even accused her mother of lying and trying to use a baby to force him into marriage.

Aspen grabbed jeans and a shirt and dressed, then wrapped her arms around herself. She'd been afraid of the same thing.

Afraid to trust that Dylan might love her.

She had to make him understand that her fears stemmed from her past.

She hurried through the bedroom door into the living room, then to the door. But just as she opened it, she spotted Dylan lying on the ground, facedown, not moving.

Panic sent a bolt of adrenaline through her, and she screamed, and turned to run inside to phone for help. But a big, hard body tackled her from behind, and she pitched forward, then they rolled backward. Her knees hit the steps, her hands clawing for control and digging into gravel and dirt.

Two hands jerked her by the shoulders, and she scrambled to try to escape, but a hard whack on the back of her neck made her reel with pain. Her head spun, the world shifted in a drunken state of nausea, and an icy chill invaded her as the man dragged her up and threw her over his shoulder.

He stalked down the hill, rocks scattering and pinging off the ridge as he wove through the brush to an old van.

She kicked at him and pounded his back with her fists, but he threw her inside and slapped her across the face so hard that her eyes sank back in her head and she passed out.

Sometime later, she aroused from unconsciousness, terror sweeping over her. Her hands and legs were bound with tight-corded ropes, her mouth gagged, and the van was bumping over gravel and dirt.

Who was this man?

And where was he taking her?

DYLAN SLOWLY ROUSED from the black sea where he'd fallen, swimming upward toward the light. He had to paw his way up, had to surface.

Aspen needed him.

He pushed up from the ground, his hands scraping the dry brush as he sat up and tried to regain his senses.

Then he spotted the piece of thunderwood.

Pure panic slammed into him. How long had he been out? Did Turnbull have Aspen or was it a copycat?

Fear made him shoot upward, and he staggered up

the steps, and rushed inside, his gaze scanning the darkened interior.

Pausing to listen, he prayed that she was still alive. Still inside somewhere.

But he inched through the living room to the bedroom and found it empty.

Jack.

God, please don't let him have hurt the baby.

Trembling with terror, he raced to the second bedroom and held his breath as he checked inside. A whimper from the crib made his chest clench, and he flipped on the light and hurried toward the crib.

Jack had stirred and opened his eyes and was looking up at him as if he knew something was wrong.

He quickly checked the baby for injuries, but he appeared to be all right.

Though his mind raced with horrid images of what this man might be doing to Aspen, he shoved the images aside. He had to act fast.

Turnbull had kept his other victims for at least twenty-four hours. But what if this was the copycat?

And if Turnbull had killed his mother so violently and was escalating, what would he do to Aspen?

Cold sweat broke out on his brow.

"I'll be right back, Jack. I have to get help." His heart pounding, he raced to the bedroom and retrieved his gun and phone. Throwing on his shirt, he punched in Tom's phone number. Three rings later and Tom answered.

"Tom, it's Dylan. Either Turnbull or his copycat found us and he has Aspen."

"I'll call the locals and tell them to set up roadblocks and get some choppers in the air."

"We need to figure out where he'd take her. And I need someone to watch Jack."

"I'll call Miguel right now."

Dylan scrubbed his hand over his face, frantic. He had to think. Where would Turnbull take Aspen?

Dear God, please don't let me be too late….

ASPEN'S BODY ACHED from being tossed around in the back of the van as the vehicle careened over the rocky terrain. The interior was pitch-black, the smell of cigarette, sweat and booze an acrid stench that made bile rise to her throat. Was Dylan all right?

Was he alive?

Panic clogged her throat and she tried desperately to choke back the fear.

What if he didn't find her in time?

And what if he was dead and Jack was in that house all alone? No one would even know he was there.

Who would take care of him if she didn't survive?

Emma.

Emma would raise Jack as her own. Emma knew what it was like to lose a mother. She would tell him about Aspen and about how they grew up together on the reservation. She would share the stories that Aspen wanted so badly to pass on to her son.

And even though Emma was only half Ute, she would raise him in the Ute way.

Tears leaked down her eyes, but she was helpless to stop them. She didn't want to leave Jack again—she'd promised him she wouldn't.

She didn't want to die, either. She wanted to watch

Jack grow up. Teach him how to ride a bike. Watch him grow into a man.

And she wanted to tell Dylan that she loved him.

She sobbed with the realization. Why hadn't she realized it before? Why hadn't she confessed her feelings?

Confess how terrified she'd been that he couldn't love her back? That that was the reason she had stopped trying to contact him.

She'd tried to convince herself that having Jack was enough. That she didn't need or want Dylan.

But she'd lied to herself for months.

And now it was too late.

The van suddenly screeched to a halt, and her stomach knotted with a sick fear as the sound of the driver's door opening and slamming rent the night.

Outside the van, footsteps shuffled against rock. Somewhere in the distance, an animal screeched.

Then hard bands of steel snapped around her wrists and dragged her from the van. She kicked again, determined to fight, but he slammed his fist against her cheek and she saw stars.

Then he dragged her across the rocky terrain toward some kind of small building a few feet away.

A church.

She blinked, trying to focus. It was old, weathered, deserted. Overgrown weeds and bushes shrouded the front. The smell of something rotten permeated the air.

And the scent of death floated to her, eerie and numbing as the sight of several graves caught her eye.

Then the shiny blade of a knife shattered the darkness

as he tossed her against one of the cement markers staked in the dirt-packed ground.

DYLAN HAD DROPPED JACK OFF AT Emma's. She was terrified but Miguel had stayed with her to calm her, and he'd promised to call as soon as he found Aspen.

He only hoped he found her alive.

He raced into the crime-lab conference room to confer with the others.

"The ME confirmed that Ulysses Ramstead was the other dead man in the prison bus crash. He must have joined forces to help Turnbull escape, then Turnbull stabbed him in the back and left his body to burn so we would think he was dead. Turnbull left his dental plate to mislead us."

"Where would he take Aspen?" Dylan asked as he paced the room. "I would have thought if he wanted to get revenge on me, he would have just done it right there. That he would have even forced me to watch."

"He does want revenge," Ben said. "But his sickness has to do with killing Ute women."

"That's right," Tom said. "Remember his profile. He hated his mother because she raised him on the reservation. Because she was brutal and a religious zealot."

Dylan fisted his hands, his heart hammering. He had to climb in Turnbull's head. Think like the sadistic sick man he was.

Turnbull hated his mother and he'd killed her. He hated Ute women.

He hated the church.

His mind racing, he hurried to the table and opened up the files on Turnbull, quickly scanning them.

"Send someone to Turnbull's mother's house. Maybe he's going to take her there."

"I'll cover the house," Tom said.

Dylan hesitated, his mind humming with another possibility. "He knows we'll look there, though."

Dylan flipped the page, scanning the psychologist's notes. "This is it. The church." He glanced up at Tom with dread in his belly. "You go to his house, and I'll check out the church. He might take her to the very place his mother forced him to go as a child when she pounded religion into him."

Tom gave a clipped nod. "You might be right."

Both men sprang into action, Tom hurrying to his car and Dylan to his own.

He flipped on his siren, spread the map on the car seat and tore from the crime lab, weaving his way through Kenner City, out of town.

Bright lights nearly blinded him from an oncoming car, and he blew his horn, then sped past, careening around a curve, his hands sweating on the steering wheel and his breathing choppy.

It seemed like days, but was only a matter of minutes until he reached the small dilapidated, deserted church where Turnbull had been baptized.

He spotted a dark van, and his heart thundered. He had to be in time.

Aspen couldn't be dead.

He had to save her and take her home to their son.

Not bothering to slow down, he screeched to a halt, jumped out, his gun at the ready.

The blue lights twirled across the barren land, flickering across the terrifying scene in front of him.

Aspen was on her knees in the dirt by a marker, her hands tied, feet bound, while Turnbull stalked around her, preaching a sermon as he wielded the Ute ceremonial knife.

Chapter Nineteen

Aspen shuddered at the sound of the crazed man humming in the ancient language. He didn't look Ute, but he seemed entranced at the moment, as some kind of demon had possessed his soul.

The scent of death, damp soil and fear invaded her. Her head throbbed where he'd hit her, and her wrists and ankles were raw from trying to free herself from the ropes biting into her skin.

She was going to die.

No, she'd heard the siren. The police were coming.

Dylan would find her and save her before this madman used his knife on her.

He leapt toward her, jamming the pointed blade at her throat, and she flinched as a droplet of blood seeped from her impaled skin.

Then a loud growl broke the silence, the sound almost inhuman, and she looked up and saw Dylan launch himself at Frank Turnbull.

She screamed, fighting to escape her bindings, fear clutching her as her captor swung the knife in a wide arc, then jabbed the point at Dylan.

Dylan shouted an obscenity, and threw his body against Turnbull's and the two men fell to the ground in battle.

It was so dark she couldn't see, but the scent of blood assaulted her, and Dylan's shout of pain rent the air.

Dear God, no. Dylan couldn't die. She needed him.

And so did their son.

RAGE SEARED DYLAN, more painful than the blade that Turnbull drove into his shoulder. Blood oozed from the wound, trickling down his arm, but he ignored the pain, and grabbed Turnbull's hand, then they fought for the weapon.

Turnbull must have been working out in prison, and had gained weight and muscle, but the images of the women he had brutally slain flashed back, fueling Dylan's fury and renewing his strength.

He karate chopped Turnbull's wrist and the knife flew to the ground. Turnbull scrambled to get it, but Dylan tackled him and slammed his fist into the man's nose. Bones crunched and blood spewed, but Turnbull wasn't giving up.

He rammed his head into Dylan's stomach, gripped his arm where he'd stabbed him and pain rocked through Dylan. He grunted and fought back, but Turnbull managed to escape and grabbed the knife out of the dirt.

Aspen screamed as the man ran toward her, and Dylan saw red.

Adrenaline surged through him, and he reached for his gun. He found it on the ground by a cement marker, picked it up and aimed.

The bullet pierced Turnbull in the back, and he

howled, then twisted around with a shocked gleam in his eyes as if he'd never expected Dylan to actually win.

Then Turnbull dove toward him again and Dylan pumped another round into the man. His body bounced backward, and he collapsed on top of a grave.

A sinister smile tilted his lips and his mouth moved. "I knew you were just like me," he said in a croaked whisper.

"I'm nothing like you," Dylan growled.

Turnbull's body jerked, then he took his last breath and his body went still.

Dylan staggered to him, then kicked the knife from his hand. Aspen cried his name, and he turned to see her struggling to free herself from the bindings.

He stumbled across the dirt-packed grave, then fell to his knees.

Moonlight streaked her pale face, and rage shot through him again as he spotted the bruise on her cheek and forehead.

"Are you all right?"

She nodded, tears streaming down her face. "But you're hurt."

"I've had worse," he said. Then he cursed as he looked down at her bound limbs.

A fierce frown pulled at his mouth as he retrieved Turnbull's knife, cut the ropes binding her wrists, then hastily slashed the ones on her ankles.

She fell against him on a sob, and he wrapped his arms around her.

"You're safe now," he whispered hoarsely. Relief ebbed through him as his blood soaked her blouse and they clung together. "I'm sorry I left you. Sorry he got to you—"

She cupped his face between her hands. "Shh. No, it's okay. It's over now."

"Thank God you're alive," he said.

They clung to each other for a long time, but she finally insisted on calling an ambulance. While they waited, she helped him tie his T-shirt around the wound to stop the blood flow.

He leaned against her, his pallor gray and chalky, and fear clutched Aspen. She had to be honest with Dylan.

He had nearly died to save her life.

He might leave again, even if she did confess her feelings, but she had to take that chance. Whether he loved her not, she wanted Jack to know this courageous strong man.

She wanted him to have the father she never had.

"I love you, Dylan," Aspen whispered. "I'm sorry I didn't tell you about Jack."

He gazed into her eyes, a mixture of hurt and hope glimmering in his slow smile.

"I'm just sorry you didn't trust me," he said gruffly. "I would never have tried to separate you from our son."

Her heart fluttered with anticipation, love mushrooming inside her as he fused his mouth with hers.

"And I love you, too," he whispered. "I think I did from the moment I saw you."

Epilogue

Two days later, the team met in the conference room at the Kenner County Crime Unit to review the case.

Tom had located Turnbull's half brother, Freddy, who'd gone into hiding when he found out his half sibling could have escaped.

"We've identified the woman's body we found in the river. She was just an innocent Turnbull killed for fun."

Dylan gritted his teeth. "What about Watts and Perkins?" Dylan asked. "Do we have any leads?"

"They didn't take the bait and come for Aspen," Tom said. "Which makes me think that they've both left the reservation."

"They're probably long gone, in Mexico now," Tom said.

Dylan shifted, although his nerves spiked at the thought that they might return for Aspen. He wouldn't allow them to. Not now.

Not ever.

"We did link Lightfoot to the Wayne family," Ben said. "He admitted he took money to help his people, and that he was afraid they'd call in his marker. He's agreed to go into Witness Protection. I think he's afraid of what they might have asked him to do."

Dylan gave a clipped nod. He was glad to see the man go.

Not that he thought Aspen was in love with Lightfoot. In spite of the pain and stitches in his shoulder, the past two days had been bliss.

"Before everyone leaves," Tom cut in, "Callie and I have an announcement."

Callie grinned and took Tom's hand in hers. "We're engaged."

Congratulations erupted all the way around with hugs and handshaking.

"It looks as if my brother's getting married, too," Dylan said as he clapped Tom on the back. "He called earlier to say he and Emma have eloped to Las Vegas."

They wrapped up the meeting, and Dylan hurried toward his car and drove back to Aspen's. The sight of her pueblo-style house brought a smile to his face and a sense of peace over him.

Aspen had worried that he wouldn't want to live on the reservation and had surprised him by offering to move, but he wanted his son to be raised in his mother's footsteps and to appreciate his culture.

His heart warmed as he parked, walked up to the door and let himself in. She smiled at him and Jack cooed as he rushed over to give them both a kiss.

Aspen was right. This was home. But it had nothing to do with the house.

It was home because the two people he loved most in the world were here.

And soon he would make Aspen his wife, then his son would carry on his name. And no one would ever tear them apart again.

* * * * *

KENNER COUNTY CRIME UNIT
continues in Harlequin Intrigue with
PULLING THE TRIGGER, next month
from Julie Miller!

In honor of our 60th anniversary, Harlequin® American Romance® is celebrating by featuring an all-American male each month, all year long with MEN MADE IN AMERICA! *This June, we'll be featuring American men living in the West.*

Here's a sneak preview of THE CHIEF RANGER by Rebecca Winters.

Chief Ranger Vance Rossiter has to confront the sister of a man who died while under Vance's watch…and also confront his attraction to her.

"Chief Ranger Rossiter?" The sight of the woman who'd stepped inside Vance's office brought him to his feet. "I'm Rachel Darrow. Your secretary said I should come right in."

"Please," he said, walking around his desk to shake her hand. At a glance he estimated she was in her mid-twenties. Her feminine curves did wonders for the pale blue T-shirt and jeans she was wearing. "Ranger Jarvis informed me there's a young boy with you."

The unfriendly expression in her beautiful green eyes caught him off guard. "Yes," was her clipped reply. "When we arrived in Yosemite the ranger told me I couldn't go anywhere in the park until I talked to you first."

"That's right."

"Knowing you wanted this meeting to be private, he offered to show my nephew around Headquarters."

So this woman was the victim's sister… "What's his name?"

"Nicky."

The boy who haunted Vance's dreams now had a name. "How old is he?"

"He turned six three weeks ago. Were you the man in charge when my brother and sister-in-law were killed?"

"Yes. To tell you I'm sorry for what happened couldn't begin to convey my feelings."

The woman's gaze didn't flicker. "I won't even try to describe mine. Just tell me one thing. Was their accident preventable?"

"Yes," he answered without hesitation.

"In other words, the people working under you fell asleep on your watch and two lives were snuffed out as a result."

Hearing it put like that, he had to set the record straight. "My staff had nothing to do with it. I, myself, could have prevented the loss of life."

Ms. Darrow's expression hardened. "So you admit culpability."

"Yes. I take full blame."

A look of pain crossed over her features. "You can just stand there and admit it?" Her cry echoed that of his own tortured soul.

"Yes." He sucked in his breath.

"I work for a cruise line. Aboard ship, it's the captain's responsibility to maintain rigid safety regulations. If a disaster like that had happened while he was in charge he would have been relieved of his command and never given another ship again."

Rachel Darrow couldn't know she was preaching to the converted. "If you've come to the park with the intention of bringing a lawsuit against me for negligence, maybe you should." It would only be what he deserved.

"Maybe I will."

In the next instant, she wheeled around and hurried

out of his office. Vance could have gone after her, but it would cause a scene, something he was loath to do for a variety of reasons. In the first place, he needed to cool down before he approached her again.

The discovery of the Darrows' frozen bodies had affected every ranger in the park. A little boy had been orphaned—a boy whose aunt was all he had left.

* * * * *

Will Rachel allow Vance to explain—and will she let him into her heart?
Find out in
THE CHIEF RANGER
Available June 2009 from Harlequin® American Romance®.

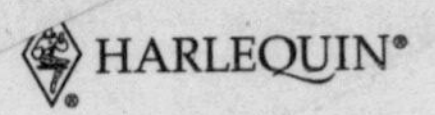

INTRIGUE®

COMING NEXT MONTH

Available June 9, 2009

#1137 BIG SKY DYNASTY by B.J. Daniels
Whitehorse, Montana: The Corbetts
The hunky ranch owner believes his deranged ex-wife is dead—until he finds out she has returned to town and wormed her way into the life of a sweet and trusting knit shop owner. He's ready to risk his life to save them both from a dangerous obsession.

#1138 PULLING THE TRIGGER by Julie Miller
Kenner County Crime Unit
A suspected murderer has escaped into the mountains, but two of Kenner County's finest are hot on his trail. The only thing hotter is the attraction that still sizzles between these former lovers. Can they catch their man and resurrect their love?

#1139 MIDNIGHT INVESTIGATION by Sheryl Lynn
The feisty skeptic is unimpressed by the tall, well-built police officer who claims psychic abilities—until she unknowingly invites a malevolent spirit home. Now the man she doubted may be the only one who can help....

#1140 HEIRESS RECON by Carla Cassidy
The Recovery Men
The former-navy SEAL is in the business of recovery, but he never figured his job would call for repossessing a beautiful heiress. He has promised her father that he will keep her safe from the threats that are being made against her life, but can he guard his heart as well?

#1141 THE PHANTOM OF BLACK'S COVE by Jan Hambright
He's a Mystery
The isolated clinic in Black's Cove holds many secrets, and the investigative journalist is ready to uncover all—until the owner's grandson tries to stop her. Can these secrets be dangerous enough to endanger both of their lives?

#1142 ROYAL PROTOCOL by Dana Marton
Defending the Crown
When the opera house he designed is overtaken by rebels, the prince stays behind to protect his masterpiece—and the beautiful young diva that is trapped with him. Surviving opening night takes on a whole new meaning as they fight for their lives.